The Oldest Orphan

The Oldest Orphan

L'Aîné des orphelins

TIERNO MONÉNEMBO

Translated by Monique Fleury Nagem

With an introduction by Adele King

University of Nebraska Press, Lincoln and London

Publication of this book was
assisted by a grant from the
National Endowment for the Arts

Library of Congress Cataloging-
in-Publication Data
Monénembo, Tierno, 1947–
[L'Aîné des orphelins. English]
The oldest orphan = L'Aîné des
orphelins / Tierno Monénembo;
translated by Monique Fleury
Nagem; with an introduction by
Adele King.   p.   cm.
ISBN 0-8032-3224-1 (cl. : alk.
paper) – ISBN 0-8032-8285-0
(pbk. : alk. paper)   I. Nagem,
Monique F., 1941– .   II. Title.
PQ3989.2.M58 A7613 2004
843′.914–dc21
2003009666

INTRODUCTION

The Rwandan Genocide

Adele King

Tierno Monénembo's novel, *The Oldest Orphan*, is part of an increasing body of literature, much of it written by Africans, about one of the major events in modern African history, the 1994 genocide in Rwanda. Most of the novel is set in the years after the genocide and describes its effects upon the narrator, who was a young child in 1994 and who is fifteen when he tells his story.

There are three ethnic groups in Rwanda, the Tutsis, the Hutus, and the Twas. All three speak the same language, Kinyarwanda, and worshipped the same god, Imana, before the arrival of Christian missionaries. Tutsis were originally owners of cattle, a major source of wealth in the Rwandan economy, while Hutus were primarily farmers. The distinctions between the Hutus and the Tutsis were initially minimal and based on occupation and wealth. The royal family was Tutsi, while the majority of the population was Hutu. There was much intermarriage and before colonization it had been possible to move from one group to the other. (The Twas – often called Pygmies – tended to remain more separate.)

In 1921 the Belgians established a mandate in Rwanda, which had been a German colony since 1894. The Belgians introduced an identity card establishing the ethnic group of each individual, a system based on such considerations as the length of the nose. The Belgians believed that the Tutsis were a superior race, of Egyptian origin, while the Hutus were considered 'Bantus,' and an inferior group. The colonial administration made the separation between Tutsis and Hutus fixed, and so began the antagonism between the two groups. Rwanda fell into what one writer has termed the 'ethnic trap,' set by ethnologists and missionaries, and maintained by Hutu leaders who wanted power and encouraged a growing tension between the minority that had ruled the country and the majority.

The stage for the 1994 genocide in Rwanda had been set many

years earlier. In 1959 the last great Tutsi king died under mysterious circumstances. Revolts by Hutu peasants followed, the beginning of the bloodbaths referred to in the novel. Twenty thousand Tutsis were massacred. This provoked the exodus of hundreds of thousands of Tutsis, primarily to Uganda and Burundi.

In 1961 Rwanda became independent; the first legislative elections resulted in a victory for the Hutu political parties. A coup d'état in 1973 brought Juvénal Habyarimana, also a Hutu, to power. He was elected president in 1978. Continued attacks by Hutus on Tutsis resulted in further exodus from the country. In 1990 a Tutsi army, composed of forces in exile, had some military success against the government of Habyarimana, but by then the genocide was imminent, with Hutu militias armed by the French. The outside world was warned of what would happen; radio broadcasts calling for help were sent by an Italian woman, Tonia Locatelli, who was massacred by Hutu militants on March 9, 1992 (another event referred to in the novel).

A peace treaty, the Treaty of Arusha between the government and the Tutsi forces (the Front Patriotique Rwandais), was signed in 1993. The Arusha treaty, however, was a prologue to genocide, not to peace. Habyarimana was killed on April 6, 1994, in an airplane crash, under circumstances that are still unclear. By the next day government officials – Hutus who were favorable to a democratic government and were not against the Tutsis – were assassinated by Hutu militants. This massacre of Hutu moderates, including Agathe Uwilingiyimana, the prime minister, was the signal for the killing of Tutsis, by the Interahamwe (Hutu militias), which continued for one hundred days. The Hutu population had been prepared for the massacres by a propaganda campaign, particularly on the radio, in which Tutsis were compared to cockroaches that must be eliminated. At least eight hundred thousand Tutsis and some moderate Hutus were killed. Then Tutsi forces moved into the country from Uganda and succeeded in taking Kigali, the capital, on July 4 (an event referred to in the novel). Many Hutus fled the country, primarily for the Congo, where some remained at least as late as 2002. The French, who had supported the Hutu regime, sent in an armed force that helped the refugees, including many guilty of genocide, to escape.

While responsibility for the genocide lies with the Hutu regime, the United Nations forces, initially in Rwanda to ensure that the Arusha treaty would be observed, did nothing to prevent the massacres and left the country, taking most European and American nationals with them, and leaving the Tutsis to their fate. European countries with ties to Rwanda – namely, Belgium and France – did nothing, nor did the Vatican or the United States. The French president in 1994, François Mitterand, has been quoted as saying that genocides in Africa were unimportant.

More recently, the United Nations and the U.S. government have apologized for their inaction. The Belgian government has not only apologized but tried and convicted Rwandans now resident in Belgium for guilt in genocidal acts. Those convicted include two Rwandan nuns.[1]

FEST'AFRICA

A few years after the genocide in Rwanda, Tierno Monénembo was invited, along with nine other writers from various countries in Francophone Africa, to participate in a project organized by Fest'Africa: 'Rwanda: écrire par devoir de mémoire' (Writing so as not to forget). The organizers, led by Nocky Djedanoum from Chad, felt that Africans had too often been silent about the events of the genocide. The writers went to Rwanda in 1998 to participate in a residency and to show their moral solidarity with the people of Rwanda. The Oldest Orphan is Monénembo's contribution to the Fest'Africa project. It was awarded the Prix Tropiques by the French Agency for Development in 2000.

Monénembo described his reactions to this project in an article in Libération, a French daily newspaper, in 1999.[2] In 1976, while studying in Lyon, one of his friends was from Rwanda, a country about which he knew little. 'I even mixed up the words, saying Hutsi and Tutshu, Urundi and Buranda.' Later, in 1992, he met Alice, a young woman born in Zaire, from a Rwandan family, who was studying law in France; she introduced him to Rwandan culture through music. In 1998, when he went to Rwanda, he met Alice again. She was working for the international penal tribunal, having returned to Rwanda shortly after the Tutsi troops entered Kigali. As Monénembo mentions how he thought of using her experience for a novel, it is probable that the character of Claudine is partly inspired by Alice. In Rwanda Monénembo met other writers on the Fest'Africa project and also Guineans who had escaped from the regime of Sékou Touré to become shopkeepers in Kigali. For Monénembo, in exile in Europe since 1973, talking with other Africans, without the presence of Europeans, was a salutary experience. He admired Rwandan culture, claiming in an interview that Rwanda is socially more advanced than France.[3]

Most participants in the Fest'Africa program have published a book about the genocide.[4] A Cameroonian filmmaker made a documentary film about the project. Bruce Clarke, a South African artist, is developing a Garden of Memory, in which stones are placed in remembrance of those who died. Rwandan participants in the project have published several essays but have found it more difficult to write fiction. Monénembo commented that there were certain events in his native Guinea, at the time of Sékou Touré's prison camps, that he could not use as subjects for fiction.

Two of the writers, Véronique Tadjo and Abdourahman A. Waberi, whose books contain short stories and essays, comment on how hard it was to begin to write. They often speak of the horrors they saw. Several of the writers are highly critical of the political position of western governments, the United Nations, and the Catholic Church. Waberi, for instance, tells a story, only slightly fictionalized, about a woman who keeps and feeds a dog that had eaten the bodies of members of her family. She calls the dog Minuar, the French abbreviation for the United Nations forces, to recall the UN forces that did nothing to save lives.

TIERNO MONÉNEMBO

Thierno Saïdou Diallo was born in Fouta-Djallon, Guinea, in 1947. Monénembo is his pen name, which he derived from the name of his grandmother, Néné Mbo, an important influence on his childhood. Monénembo's native language was Fulani. He lived in a small village of six thousand, Poredaka, which was visited in 1958–60 by many African Americans looking for their 'roots.'

Guinea, under the leadership of Sékou Touré, was the only Francophone African country to vote in 1958 against de Gaulle's offer of association with France. When it became the first country in French West Africa to gain independence, France immediately withdrew all its colonial officials and all aid. As a young man, Monénembo was initially in favor of Sékou Touré and supported him until 1964, when the situation worsened considerably and Touré established a cruel tyranny. Monénembo escaped from Guinea in 1969 by walking one hundred miles through the bush. At first he went to Senegal, where he studied medicine for a year, then to Abidjan, in the Côte d'Ivoire, where he studied biochemistry (1970–73). At that time he began a novel, which he never finished.[5]

In 1973 Monénembo went to France, first to Grenoble, then to Lyon, where he earned a doctorate in biochemistry (1979). His first novel, *Les crapauds-brousse*, appeared at the beginning of 1979. He had sent it to the Editions du Seuil, one of the most prestigious French publishing houses, without any of the usual contacts writers establish. *Les crapauds-brousse* (translated as *The Bush Toads*, the only novel by Monénembo in English translation before *The Oldest Orphan*) is set in an unnamed country, presumably Guinea under Sékou Touré, and is based partly on Monénembo's own escape.

Monénembo did various odd jobs in Lyon to support himself, as he had no scholarship. Eventually he was employed as an assistant, and later he taught in St. Etienne, Algeria, and Morocco before moving to Normandy, where he has lived since 1985. He quit teaching in 1990 to devote himself to writing. By then he had published *Les écailles du ciel* (The shells of the sky, 1986), which won the Grand Prix de l'Afrique Noire. Like *Les crapauds-brousse*, *Les écailles du ciel* is also set in Guinea and is a bitter picture of colonial and postcolonial politics.

In 1991 Monénembo's third novel, *Un rêve utile*, appeared. It is set in Lyon, where Monénembo had studied. The Guinean hero works as a deliveryman for household appliances while pursuing his studies, as Monénembo did in Lyon. The story is told in continual circles of events between Lyon and Guinea, to give the reader a feeling of the shock of an exile moving from one city to the other. *Un attiéké pour Elgass* (A fish feast for Elgass, 1993), Monénembo's fourth novel, is set in Abidjan, Côte d'Ivoire, among the Guinean exile community, with whom Monénembo had lived for several years. Moving away from settings in Africa, Monénembo wrote *Pelourinho* (1995), the story of an African, Escritoire ('the writer'), looking for the history of his family among the inhabitants of the former slave colony in Brazil (where Monénembo spent six months). As occurs often in his work, the story is told indirectly through one or more narrators. The use of narrative voices to tell the story is, he has said, a link to African oral legends. The novel was partly inspired by Monénembo's fascination with the African diaspora in the New World, a fascination that began when as a child he saw African Americans visiting his village. *Cinéma* (1997) returns to Guinea and the year of Guinean independence, 1958. The story is told through the eyes of an adolescent boy, who sometimes imagines himself as the hero of a Western film. As in *The Oldest Orphan* the political events are seen indirectly through the eyes of a young narrator.

Monénembo's novels describe the painful history of postindependence Africa, although he has said that he knows that literature can never teach lessons, that 'one always writes in vain.' He is working on several novels relating the history of the Fulani people (the *Peuhl*, in French).

Monénembo's style includes much punning and word play. (He has cited Rabelais as an author he particularly admires.) His novels before *The Oldest Orphan* are difficult, without straightforward chronologies, often with narratives in reverse. Such work disrupts our normal reading habits. If his work is often critical, particularly of African intellectuals, there is humor and sympathy for his characters, especially common people, many of whom are living under tyrannical political regimes or in exile. He has said that his characters are obsessed with memory, for they have a heavy, unbearable past.

THE OLDEST ORPHAN

The Oldest Orphan (2000) is Monénembo's most accessible work, though often similar to his earlier novels in its use of a narrator, who does not always keep his reader informed of what has happened, and in the plot, which jumps back and forth in time. If many of the characters in his previous novels suffer from tragic events related to the history of their countries, Faustin, the narrator of *The Oldest Orphan*, has a past so heavy that he seems unable even to recall it.

In comparison to most Fest'Africa writing, Monénembo's novel is less directly about the events of 1994. The genocide is always there but seldom directly described until the final pages of the novel. He has said that he needed to have some distance from the events. He could not be a witness or a journalist. He wanted to make the experience more human, even to add a bit of humor.[6] There is, for example, the humorous episode when Rodney and Faustin, both cynical observers of tragedy, fool the BBC reporters into believing Faustin's many invented stories about the death of his parents.

Some events in *The Oldest Orphan* are based on reality. Tonia Locatelli, the Italian woman butchered in 1992 by the Hutu militia for her attempts to warn the outside world of the coming genocide, becomes a neighbor of Faustin's family. The Caritas Bookshop, where Faustin guards cars belonging to the nongovernmental organizations, still exists in Kigali. When Faustin describes the bodies of pregnant women impaled on bits of wood, this alludes to a woman whose body became an image throughout the world for the horror of the genocide. She was raped for several days, before a bit of wood was thrust into her vagina and she was killed with a machete blow to her neck. (This woman, named Immaculée or Mukandori, becomes the Queen, the narrative voice in Koulsy Lamko's novel, *La phalène des collines* [2002], where she turns into a butterfly after her death.)

The description of the massacre in the church at Nyamata is very close to what happened. A BBC reporter who visited Nyamata in June 1994 recalls seeing the ground inside the church 'thick with bodies – in places, three or four deep.' 'It was clear from the sheer number of corpses in the church that the victims had gathered there because they thought it would provide them with shelter.'[7]

Monénembo includes, however, many made-up events, among them the convent of Brazilian nuns, perhaps included because of Monénembo's visit to Brazil and his interest in the community of those of African descent in the New World, the subject of his novel *Pelourinho*. (There are other echoes of Monénembo's earlier work in *The Oldest Orphan*, including Faustin's love of watching Western films in the Fraternity Bar, which is a favorite pastime of Binguel in *Cinéma*.)

Faustin tells his story in a seemingly hard, cynical tone without illusions; he is fifteen when he is condemned to death, but already old in his knowledge of the evil of men, while still a child in other ways, as can be seen from his vocabulary, his misunderstanding of many words he hears. Many Rwandans, rather than directly saying 'the genocide' or 'the massacre,' refer to 'the events' (*les événements*); Faustin refers to 'the advents' (*les avènements*). He is blasé, evoking horrors without much sentiment. As Monénembo has commented, 'Once innocence is lost nothing remains.'[8]

During Faustin's trial there are many echoes of Camus's *L'Étranger*. Like Meursault, Faustin is a stranger in a world that considers him a monster. He has become incapable of understanding the society around him. His only pleasures are physical, but when condemned to death, just as Meursault can forget Marie, he can forget Claudine. He has no sense of regret for what he has done. The horror of the massacre at Nyamata, a memory he has tried to suppress, has changed him so profoundly that any attempt at morality becomes meaningless. Faustin's 'monstrosity,' however, has explicit causes. He kills a friend whom he caught having sex with his young sister. His defense of his family is only fully comprehensible after his trial, when he describes his close ties to his family and the death of his parents. At the conclusion of the novel, his mother might be seen as like the pelican, an allegorical symbol of Christ, giving life with her own blood.[9] The Oldest Orphan, like L'Étranger, ends with an evocation of a mother, and the reconciliation of her son to the world of emotion.

NOTES

1. I am indebted for some information to an excellent essay by a Rwandan who grew up in exile and returned to his country after the genocide. Benjamin Sehene, Le piège ethnique (Paris: Dagorno, 1999).

   A short bibliography of books in English on the genocide includes: Alison Des Forges, Leave None to Tell the Story (New York: Human Rights Watch, 1999); Alain Destexhe, Rwanda and Genocide in the Twentieth Century, trans. Alison Marschner (New York: New York University Press, 1995); Philip Gourevitch, We Wish to Inform You That Tomorrow We Will Be Killed with Our Families (New York: Farrar, Straus, Giroux, 1998); Fergal Keane, Season of Blood: A Rwandan Journey (New York: Viking, 1995); and Gérard Prunier, The Rwanda Crisis: History of a Genocide (New York: Columbia University Press, 1995). Also highly recommended is a film, available on video: Chronicle of a Genocide Foretold, written and directed by Daniele Lacourse and Yan Patry (New York: First Run/Icarus Films, 1996).

2. 'Rendez-vous au café L'Eden sans passer par l'Europe,' Libération (May 13, 1999; http://liberation.com/livres/99mai/0513rwanda.html (September 19, 2000).

3. 'Le Rwanda: Le désire de mémoire' (interview with Rodney Saint-Eloi), Boutures 1, no. 3 (September 2000), 4–7; http://www.lehman.cuny.edu/ile.en. ile/boutures/0103/entretien.html (August 4, 2002).

4. Books published in French include

NOVELS AND STORIES: Boubacar Boris Diop (Senegal), *Murambi, le livre des ossements* (Paris: Stock, 2000); Monique Ilboudo (Burkina Faso), *Murekatete* (Genevilliers: Le Figuier, 2000); Koulsy Lamko (Chad), *La phalène des collines* (Paris: Serpent à Plumes, 2002); Véronique Tadjo (Côte d'Ivoire), *L'ombre d'Imana* (Paris: Actes Sud, 2000); Abdourahman A. Waberi (Djibouti), *Terminus* (Paris: Serpent à Plumes, 2000);

POETRY: Nocky Djedanoum (Chad), *Nyamirambo* (Genevilliers: Le Figuier, 2000);

ESSAYS: Vénuste Kayimahé, *France-Rwanda, les coulisses du génocide* (Paris: Dagorno, 2001); Jean-Marie Vianney Rurangwa, *Le génocide des Tutsi expliqué à un étranger* (Genevilliers: Le Figuier, 2000).

5. Some biographical information is based on my interview with Tierno Monénembo in 1995 and on later correspondence with him.

6. Monénembo's comment at a seminar in Paris on the genocide, November 2000.

7. 'Remembering the Victims of Nyamata,' *http://new.bbc.co.uk/1/hi/despatches /82978.stm* (August 4, 2002).

8. Interview with Rodney Saint-Eloi in *Boutures*.

9. I am indebted to a student in my course on Rwanda at Ball State University in 2002, Andrew Gaub, for his insight about the pelican.

The Oldest Orphan

While the reality of the
Rwandan genocide cannot be
denied, the situations and the
characters in this novel are,
for the most part, fictitious.

This novel was written under
the auspices of the project
Writing So As Not to Forget,
conceived by the organization Arts et Medias d'Afrique
and supported by the
Fondation de France.

Its title was suggested to me
by a Rwandan friend.

The pain of others is bearable.
Rwandan proverb

You kill a man, you're a murderer.
You kill millions, you're a conqueror.
You kill them all, you're a god.
Edmond Rostand

In memory of Issata,

For Clément,

for Jean Mukimbiri,

for the good doctor Rufuku,

for Alice, Valentine, and Laetitia

the three tigresses of Kigali whose beauty

and strength were able to repel death.

For the Rwandans, Twas, Hutus, or Tutsis . . .

alive, preferably.

I don't blame fate. I blame Thaddeus. I'm doomed. They're coming to kill me tomorrow or perhaps the day after. Even those who don't believe in God forgive before they die. But Thaddeus is unforgivable. He's the cause of all my woes.

Thaddeus is my cousin. His family's hill rose above Lake Bihira. During the rainy season, we call it *itumba*. I used to meet him there to hunt ground squirrel and carve *igisoro* games we'd sell to the tourists.[1] A few days before the plane came down, I got a message from Uncle Sentama at the weekly Bugesera market (since the last bloodbath he lives on the other side of Lake Cyambwe, in a country called Tanzania). 'Come, son of my sister,' he said. 'I need help planting sweet potatoes and taros. And if you're polite and if you do a good job, I'll take you to town to see a movie. Then I'll sew some brand new clothes for you and buy you the bicycle I've been promising you after I've sold my guinea fowl.' But there was Thaddeus, with a nose that can smell trouble and big ears that can hear everything. 'Good idea!' he crowed. 'I'm going with you. That way I'll get a bicycle too and I'll get to see Uncle Sentama again.' The messenger was one of those cattle merchants who drive their herds through the bush on both sides of the border. He had been told to take me with him the next morning at dawn. 'Not so fast!' Thaddeus declared. 'We have to get ready. What if we left on Tuesday instead? That's the day Misago the policeman does his rounds. We'll hitch a ride to Nyarubuyé in his jeep. There we'll join a group of peddlers and cross the border undisturbed. I'll talk to my father. Misago can't tell him no.' 'Tuesday, that's too long; Uncle Sentama will worry!' I tried to reason with him. But it was written in the sky that his mouth would always prevail over mine. 'Only six days!

1. A variation of the African game mancala, which is thought to be the oldest game in the world. – Trans.

I really think that's best. Come on, go tell Uncle Théoneste and Aunt Axelle good-bye. See you Tuesday morning early near the big kapok tree.' He waved good-bye and disappeared into the bamboo grove. If someone had told me, 'You'll never see your cousin Thaddeus again!' I would have called him a liar. Yet three days later, the president's plane was brought down. And then, the *advents*.[2]

⋆ ⋆

My name is Faustin, Faustin Nsenghimana. I'm fifteen years old. I'm in a cell in the Kigali central prison. I'm waiting to be executed. I was living with my parents in the village of Nyamata when the *advents* began. I can't keep from thinking back on those days. And each time I do, I tell myself I had just turned ten for nothing.

⋆ ⋆

According to Funga the witch doctor, President Habyarimana's soul must have cursed Rwanda as it left this world. Funga the witch doctor is a liar; Rwanda has been cursed for a long time. And in fact he knew that perfectly well. He was hard on the country, even during the days when everything seemed to be going well. He would malign it when the men met for drinks. 'The devil is all around here!' he'd exclaim. 'His fire is in our mountains; his cruelty in our hearts. We never know where it comes from, but with each new season blood gushes from everywhere flooding our hills and lakes. We wouldn't mind having a sea but not this color! Poor Rwanda! They call it a paradise! But it's more like hell!' He had gained much respect in the village when he cured young Gatoto of his madness and the cobbler Musaré of his paralysis. Nevertheless, I didn't like him much. I had been exhorted to adore Christ and to mistrust witch doctors. I was the one who assisted at Mass. Father Manolo had taught me to read the Holy Scriptures and to say some 'Our Fathers' to protect myself from pagan devils like him who still haunted the village a hundred years after the white man arrived! Still, I'd tremble when I saw him

---

2. In French, *avénements* (advents); the narrator describes the genocide in Rwanda using this word rather than the more common *événements* (events). – Trans.

6

handling his turtle skulls and antelope horns. Now that my fate is sealed, nothing can make me tremble.

His hut was at the other end of the village, amid the ferns and the acacias. Sometimes my mother would send me there with a bowl of cooked bananas or guinea-fowl eggs so he could read her fortune. All I have to do is close my eyes and I can still see, as if it were real, the hovel in question with its onion-shaped top and its rough red clay walls. The hardest part is to imagine Funga still in there. Perhaps it's because I saw him among the refugees trying to reach Zaire that day he offered me some smoke-dried meat. I don't remember where that was: Muhazi, Rutongo, Kayonza, or some suburb of Kigali? After hiding in so many places as I had been doing, how could I remember? The image was blurry; too many ghosts and shadowy zones around him, and nature reflects so many colors that it could have been another world. But it was definitely Funga with his rattan cane, his chapped feet, his filed teeth and a panther-skin pouch over his shoulder.

'Let's go!' he said. 'Over there, behind the banana grove! . . . Look, I still have some smoke-dried venison, some manioc, and some groundnuts. Eat up and stay out of sight! Or they might eat you because most of them haven't swallowed anything but their saliva for more than a week.'

I made quick work of the food he gave me. I relaxed; the column had moved off toward the hills.

'Come on!' he said.

'I'm waiting for my father and my mother.'

'Forget your father, forget your mother! When things are what they are, you can't think about your father or mother, you think about saving your skin!'

'I won't go without them.'

'I'll say that you're one of us! Your father and your mother . . . don't tell me you don't know!'

'Why leave? There's no more milk anywhere else!'

'Here, the gods have become heartless. There must be some luck left on the other side of Lake Kivu. But you never listen to me. That white father corrupted your head. You don't believe in Funga's powers anymore, and that'll be your ruin. Why do you think you're still alive? And why am I here standing before you, free of cholera and without any scratches? By chance? Ha ha!'

'I know where my parents are. They're hiding in a cave around Byumba, not far from Uganda. Go south, Funga, but I must head north!'

'The world has gone mad, but it's not as bad off as you are. No one dares go up there anymore, except gorillas and war mongers. I repeat, come with me! You're safer with a group; before they can reach you, they have to exterminate those around you. It's better than to be all alone.'

'If I can just find my parents, everything will be fine.'

'Faustin! Don't make me cry at my age. Believe me, there'll be nothing there but volcano ash and the misdeeds of hypocrites. As I said to the whole village: this country is going to its ruin; that's what the gods have been wanting. Everyone laughed in my face. Well, let them laugh now, if they can! I told them that soon there'll be signs from heaven. And sure enough, first the white father died. Where? In the Kabwayi Cathedral! Live, on TV and at the pope's feet! A year earlier, there had been a meningitis epidemic, and he didn't die. His car ran off the road on the way to Ngenda during the *intore* festival, and he didn't die.[3] No, he waited for the pope's visit! That's not a sign? Huh? Then there's the Italian woman who was killed in front of her own house. Everyone knew she was going to die, and no one did anything. She knew what was going to happen. She had asked for help on the French radio, on the American radio, on the Dutch radio, and no one did anything. One night, the dogs came, armed with machetes and clubs. She tried to flee toward the church. They caught up with her in the courtyard. They hacked her to pieces, and they left her to bleed to death on the graveled path, and no one made a move to help. Isn't that a sign also?'

'I've never doubted your powers! But I want to see my parents again!'

'Oh, not again. I don't believe you've lost your mind; you just want to make fun of me. In the old days, I would have made you blind or turned you into a hunchback. But it's not worth the effort anymore; it would be so insignificant compared to what's happening to us. Farewell. I'm going to join the others!'

'Here everyone knows of your charms and your beard. But over there . . .'

3. Traditional dancers.

'Listen! You think that's thunder? No, it's gunfire. Supposedly they're going to avenge everything. And they're very near here, behind the eastern hills. They're just waiting for night to come. Get out of here while there's time. Follow me, Faustin. Don't be a fool! It's only the beginning. The really bad stuff hasn't started yet. By the way, did I tell you the legend?'

'A thousand times, Funga: no one must move the sacred rock of Kagera! The whites knew that when they deliberately moved it. That's why they conquered us, and that's why there are catastrophes.'

'Then promise me you'll put the rock of Kagera back in its place one day!'

He left. I waited a long time before leaving the banana grove. It was not because I was tired (past a certain point, anyone gets used to an inconvenience) and not because I wanted to think either (the *advents* provided enough material for that); no, I didn't want to see Funga leave, and I didn't want to cry. Suddenly I realized that from then on he was my only link with the world. 'Follow him!' a little voice inside me said. 'Walk with him! Share his meals of bark and roots! Suffer from the same diarrhea if necessary, but don't stay here all alone!' I quickly left the banana grove, but my pace slowed down near the flame tree where, a few moments earlier, the column had stopped for nature's call. I no longer had the strength or the desire to go any farther. I leaned against the tree and watched with the same childish restlessness as when I used to go to the Fraternité Bar to watch the news on TV. I could see a giant spiral gripping in its circles ferns, groves, marsh papyrus, even hilltops obscuring the horizon to the south. The men, the children, and the women didn't cough, didn't speak, didn't moan. From so far away, I could hear neither the sound of their footsteps nor the squeaking of their gourds and their pans, which, by instinct of survival, they had gathered hurriedly and carried where their body hurt least: the head, the shoulders, the underarms, the buttocks. That reminded me of the movies in the Fraternité Bar when Augustine, the owner, would turn the sound down so she could call her lover in Kigali. Funga hobbled some distance behind this ghostly column. He looked like a bead separated from an endless rosary. His old legs clearly had difficulty crossing the patches of gravel and the terraces of dead vines. However, with much effort, he leaned on his rattan cane. He was walking straight ahead, head down.

Oh, Funga! 'The days have nothing to do with men: each has its own blood,' you'd say. That day, you were no longer reading the future in the stars or in the turtle skulls but rather in the wild animal droppings mixed with mud.

★ ★

My cell has a number: fourteen. There are some thirty of us in this horrid cubbyhole wedged in between number twelve and number fifteen. Men are incorrigible. Even in the very depths of hell, they cling to their vices and their superstitions. Even here, there's distrust of the number thirteen. Perhaps we should thank them for considering our well-being! Although, where we are, it's hard to be fooled. In the Juniors' Club, we don't have a fifty-fifty chance of getting a fungal infection, tuberculosis, or a stab in the belly; we just get it, period, and usually in the first two months, and it's not rare for it to all happen to you in the same damn week. But that's how the world is – even when it tries to annihilate you, it requires structure. In fact, in order to avoid a mix up in numbers, our beautiful bachelor pad has been given a pleasant name: Juniors' Club, for the simple reason that that's where the dealers, the pimps, the parricides and the *génocidaires*, whose ages range from seven to seventeen, have been crammed.[4] It sounds better than the Banished Youths Quarters or the Penal Colony for the Irredeemables. It's a name with a pleasant ring. It makes you think of a kindergarten, a boy-scout camp or a soccer team. I played center-forward on our village soccer team. I was the one who came up with the name for our team. Our coach wanted to call it Thunder. I didn't like that (there are Thunders at every stadium in Africa, even among the cocoyam eaters from Yaoundé). Overcoming my excessive shyness for once, I jumped up from the ranks and said in my reedy voice (on that day amazingly persuasive): 'Let's call it the Juniors' Group of Nyamata, please, sir!' My playmates around me were having a good laugh. The coach hesitated a while, absentmindedly bouncing the ball, then he finally gave in. 'Juniors' Group? Why not, Faustin? We'll call it the Juniors' Group, but I want to see those scores go up!' On Sunday nights at the Fraternité Bar, I was proud when I heard the announcer say, 'And on a final note, in the 'juniors' division, let's

---

4. *Génocidaires* is the term used for the perpetrators of the genocide. – Trans.

recognize Nyamata's Juniors' Group's crushing victory (four goals to nothing!) over the Rusumo Volcanoes. Two of those goals were scored by young Faustin Nsenghimana himself.' In prison you realize that memories serve a purpose. If I've survived as long as I have, I owe it to my soccer games. By focusing my thoughts on them, I can overcome my fears and get some sleep. I share a mat with Agide, whose testicles are like porridge. When the sunlight manages to pierce through the cracks in the wall, you can see his balls floating in pus and white worms crawling between his legs. There's no way to tell whether he's crying or moaning. A wild bestial sound comes out of his gaping mouth. During the day that doesn't prevent us from playing cards, sharing cigarette butts, or threatening each other with knives, broken glass, or cobblers' awls. I'll say though, at night, like everywhere else, there's not much excitement, if you exclude the weak souls who let themselves be groped by the tough guys. And since you no longer hear the sound of cars on nearby avenue de la Justice, or the roar from the halls, or the yells from the jabirus (that's the nickname for the guards – who knows why?), Agide replaces those daytime noises all by himself.⁵ You'd think we'd be used to it by now! But there are still some excitable types who curse, bang on the wall, call poor Agide all sorts of names. I wonder why one of those brutes doesn't stab him and put an end to him once and for all. That would help everyone, including Agide himself, who is closer to the grave than the cradle. Well, no; people are tactful when it comes to the dying. It's the ones in good health, those who are full of strength, who get on their nerves. They are the ones who get abused with insults and clubs, who get murdered for no reason and castrated just to check if a knife blade is sharp enough. Like that poor Zimana! He arrived one day handsome as a cowboy and with almost perfect clothes (they still had all their buttons, and the only holes were under his arms). Right off everyone was impressed, except Ayirwanda, of course. The others looked at him and boldly conjectured and imagined things, such as his having been a FAR or an elephant hunter or a highway robber.⁶ Supposedly he'd been taken out of an overcrowded prison in the north to keep him from fomenting a mutiny. At that moment Ayirwanda got up,

5. Jabirus: large storks. – Trans.

6. Forces armées rwandaises (Rwandan Armed Forces): President Habyarimana's army.

kicking the bodies stretched out on mats so he could stand: 'Soldier, gang leader! And what else, idiots! Of course, your stupid cowardly eyes can't see what I see: this man is a stool pigeon! I don't know what amount of beans or how many meters of cloth the police gave him, but I know that he's been paid to spy on us. Is there anyone among you who'll contradict me? . . . Well, you see I'm right! Zimana, am I not right? Yes or no. Aren't you an informer and a son of a bitch besides?'

Usually, when Ayirwanda says that, even the most reckless after a brief moment of bravery bow their heads and end up by giving in. But on that day, it was different. Zimana tossed away the piece of matchstick with which he'd been picking his teeth. He took forever to unbutton his shirt and fold it – it must surely have been silk! – before placing it on the windowsill. He stepped over a dozen people and walked to the wall.

'If you're a man, come fight me, Ayirwanda! Those who bite and yell have no guts! . . . Come on, you guys, make room for us! Up against the wall!'

They fought. It was so spirited, so quick, that we began to pound on the bars to get the jabirus' attention. They opened the door so we could go out in the hall, but they were careful not to interfere with the two combatants. When he saw that the fight wasn't going in his favor, Ayirwanda rushed toward the hole where he usually hid his hashish and his bananas and pulled out his brass knuckles. But Zimana, who was as agile as he was crafty, had anticipated the move. He turned toward the wall, pulled out a brick and took out a long shiny knife.

'Come here,' he threatened, 'and I'll stick this in your belly!'

Ayirwanda didn't dare. He put his brass knuckles back in the hole, sat down at the other end of the room to catch his breath, and as a result lost his prestige and his influence. The head jabiru, who up until now seemed to enjoy the spectacle just like the others, imposed silence, whacking a man or two before announcing his sentence.

'For everyone, no window privileges for ten days – longer if I catch anyone pissing outside the slop pail again. Two days of rationed food for the combatants – longer if in the meantime the smallest fight breaks out in this room. Now, go to your mats, and I want to be able to hear a pin drop!'

Three days later, Zimana was found near the laundry room with his throat slit. Otherwise Ayirwanda's reign would have been over.

It's been three years now that I've been in Kigali's central prison having to put up with Agide's hideous cries, Ayirwanda's terror, and the mood swings of one man or another. Three years – that's about the average life span here! And life, well, it's not that it's so indispensable, but you surprise yourself protecting it even when there's not much time left. That's something I've noticed in the last five years. Before the Juniors' Club, all sorts of little trifles have happened to me, even after life had returned to normal, to use an expression heard among the lost souls at the central market. I'd tell myself that it was just a stroke of bad luck, a nightmare, that would all end soon. Well, it's still not over! And yet, I certainly thought it was the end when they removed the handcuffs, took away my shoelaces and my belt and threw me in this dungeon where night follows night and the smell of wounds follows the familiar odor of death. Here, I told myself, there's no use committing suicide. You just have to lie down and wait for it to pass.

The day after my arrival, I noticed that they all just stared at me, nudging each other in the ribs and laughing perfidiously.

'So, what're you waiting for?' Ayirwanda asked me with all the fierce sharpness he could put in his voice during extremely serious moments.

'What do you mean, what am I waiting for?'

'You all saw, didn't you, I'm not making it up!'

'The slop pail, of course!' exclaimed Matata, never so pleased as when he can play supporting cast.

'The jabiru told me it wasn't my day.'

'Oh, it's not his day!' echoed mockingly from one corner of the room to the next.

'Listen, my boy!' said Matata. 'When you're new, it's a week of chores, a sort of entrance fee, in other words!'

'I won't do it; I'm going to complain to the jabirus.'

'Yeah, yeah, he's going to complain!' they all jibed.

I shouldn't have said that. First, complain to which jabiru (there must have been hundreds among the four wings of the central building, the women's annexes, and the temporary sheds put up for the newcomers)? Suddenly, I saw them all get up, bang on their bowls and clap their hands, and improvise loud songs full of arrogance. I got it: they were doing that to avoid detection by the jabirus. Ayirwanda walked toward me with his bludgeon and his brass knuckles. I thought my eye had popped out of its socket and my ribs had splintered into little pieces. I still refused to empty the slop pail when it wasn't my turn, and I refused to submit to his sexual fancies. The others thought I was conceited, but I simply thought I was right. Even the most cowardly eyes were shining with admiration for me. I was flattered, although I knew I couldn't hold out long. No one had defied Ayirwanda, and it wasn't a little guy like me who'd start! Today, it's different. As a condemned prisoner, I've become a man. I've stolen Ayirwanda's stardom. As we say in school, I jumped a few grades. First there were the central market hoodlums, then right off the Juniors' Club tough guys, and, my word, now the firing squad! I didn't expect to rise so high. I was certain I'd die within the first weeks, or at best become Ayirwanda's slave, like young Misago, who washes his rags, pinches drugs for him in the adult halls, and takes care of his prick eaten away by fungus and crabs. Deep down a voice would say: 'Hang on, son of Théoneste! Just another day or two and you'll have croaked for good! The dead don't suffer; it's their time to recover from living.' It might have been Funga the witch doctor's voice. Now that nothing is left, neither the house where I was born nor the church tower, Funga's voice is all I have. I mustn't doubt him anymore; I'm protected by his charms. How else can I explain Claudine coming all the way here to look for me?

In truth, I had totally forgotten Claudine. She's the type of person it's better to forget. She comes up to you with a smile and such ease that, at first, you think she's making fun of you. Then you realize that, no, people like her actually exist. You almost hold it against her that she's so kind, so different from the others. You stuff yourself with her meatballs and her manioc roots, you fill your pockets with her ballpoint pens and her coins, and as a result you hold more resentment toward her than gratitude. You get to the point where you wish she'd croak too, once and for all. Why the devil did she take an interest in me? After all I'm not her husband, not her lover, and not even her pimp! To do me some good, she'd explain. And that's it; I've always found people who wanted to help me suspect. So I ran away several times. If she looked for me under the central market stalls, I'd hide behind the monument on the place de la République, in the Greek's warehouses, or in the dressing rooms at the Nyamirambo stadium. The bitch always managed to find me. She'd search me, scold me in front of the snide smiles of my pals, as if she were my mother. I'd bow my head, overwhelmed with shame. She'd bow hers too to pat my hair and forehead. I could smell her perfume and her breath, which made her breasts rise. I imagined them firm and round under the lace bra. . . . Watch it, lady, I'm no longer what you think! Ask Gabrielle, Séverine, Alphonsine! I've had them all! Of all my pals, I'm the one with the longest thing. When I'm really hard, it's longer than a big soup spoon, and it fills my hand when I'm pleasuring myself in front of the women selling banana beer. I'd really like to mount you in a real iron bed with a mosquito net and some flowered pillows, given your social rank, but that I don't dare tell you. You intrigue me, you intimidate me, and that's all you can do to Théoneste's little boy. For the other women, I'm a real man; but you think of me as a little kid, as if I were still one!

And so, one fine day, when I had decided to flush from my little head ancient history and old feelings, the loudspeaker emitted its horrible crackling. I heard voices repeating one after the other, from the hall of the condemned to the jabirus' sentry boxes: 'Faustin! Faustin! Faustin Nsenghimana! Paging a certain Faustin Nsenghimana!' Outside it was raining and the heat was suffocating; the doors had been left open so those who had the strength to roam the halls could get some cool air. It had been a long time since anyone had called me. There was still someone who remembered me; that filled me with joy. I leaped from where I was sitting and let myself be carried by the human tide. I was soon in front of the warden's office hardly realizing what was happening to me. I had run mainly because of the sound of my name – a name is so important, at least no one can take it away from you – but I hadn't wondered why I was being paged.

'First remove your hands from your pockets, you little shit!' yelled the guard. 'Yes or no, are you Faustin Nsenghimana?'

'Yes, chief, it's no one but me!'

'Then come in here!'

She was seated, her back to the door. She was talking to the warden.

'I didn't bring the gun into the cell, I swear, sir,' I mumbled.

I racked my brain, but I couldn't find another reason for this invitation to appear.

She swiveled her chair around. The face to face was sudden and unexpected. I took to my heels. Most probably I would have reached the courtyard if I hadn't been stopped by the guard in the entrance hall.

'So,' she said coming near me, 'didn't you recognize me? Or do you want to get away from me? You haven't changed much! I thought I'd find you in worse shape.'

'We do what we can to keep them in good shape, Mademoiselle Karemera, but as you can see, we'd have to put some on the roof to make a little room! Food-wise, we do what we can, and then there're Friday visits to add to the rations. . . . At least for those who still have a family. Believe me, it's no plum! And of course, I'm speaking of us in the administration! Thanks to people like you, there are still some on the outside, but for how long?'

Absorbed by my rags and my filth, she hadn't paid any attention to the warden's words. She covered her face for an instant – did she want to cry or to protect herself from my stench? When she removed her hand, she wore a youthful smile, which made her madly desirable.

'I was in Uganda or I'd have come sooner, you understand.'

'I'm going to let you have my office. Since the genocide, the words 'visitor's room' don't mean anything here anymore. Lawyers and families pile in wherever they can to speak with the prisoners. Do take your time!'

They brought me an old crate, and I sat down next to her. I was looking at the cobwebs on the ceiling and gladly let my thoughts take flight while she spoke in her soft, slightly hoarse voice.

Uganda, of course! One day she told me that she was born there. During the first bloodbath, in 1959, her parents fled through the bush and took refuge there. Her pregnant mother gave birth to her at the border, two months premature.

'I understand why you speak Kinyarwanda with an English accent.' She was offended that I'd say that.

'An English accent! All I did was be born there. My soul is from here! In fact, very early my parents saw to it that I learn everything: the language, the dance of the *intore*, the game of *igisoro*, and what beans in rancid butter is.'

I didn't give a damn, but I didn't dare say that to her either. I'd let her talk on about gorillas, lakes, hills, acacias. When nostalgia took hold of her, she'd give a real lecture on nature.

'Why have we come to this?'

The terrible and inevitable question! I think she's asked it each time we've met: in front of the post office, on the sidewalk on the rue de la Récolte, and in the empty lots around the prison (I didn't know then I'd be residing here one day). I remember that, one day, I replied angrily, 'Hey, because that's what we like! It's not the first time, if I'm not mistaken!'

'You're too tough for your age! Try not to talk like that! Don't force yourself to be like the others. If you all let yourselves go, then who'll build Rwanda?'

'I don't give a damn about Rwanda! If I'd been asked, I'd have been born somewhere else.'

'Don't say that! You'll see, we'll eventually find your parents – you did tell me they're still alive, right? – and you'll live in a real house again. In the meantime why don't you return to the City of Blue Angels?'

Those are the kinds of comments that regulated our lives. There's no reason it would change in prison! I was glad of one thing, though. Here she could no longer say to me: 'And why don't you return to the City of Blue Angels?' The most dreadful words that have ever come out of her mouth! And anyway, I had decided not to listen to her. I concentrated all my efforts on my sinister cobwebs, and I let her expound freely on the inscrutable souls of human beings and on the harsh vagaries of life, but after a long while, one sentence caught my attention.

'Sembé is dead. It happened last night at Hope Hospital. Did you know he had AIDS? AIDS, at fourteen. What's going to happen to this country?'

If she hadn't been there, I'd have hit someone. The warden, the guard, that giant jabiru we call Cerberus – I'd have hit someone! Sembé. I'll never forget his crooked legs and his pointed rodent teeth with such wide gaps you could have put a pencil lead between his canine and his front tooth! I met him in front of the Caritas Bookstore. He was sitting on the edge of the sidewalk, his legs dangling above the gutter, a slim bundle resting between his legs. I can't remember what he had in his mouth, either a toothpick or a little piece of manioc? And of course, I proceeded to bully him right away (might as well let the enemy know immediately that you can bite, just in case!), the first time we saw each other. And there he was rounding his back, the little rat, resting his chest against his bundle, then he turned toward me those beady eyes that had never known fear.

'You've grown up for nothing!'

'Meaning?'

'What if I had a gun?'

'That you bought with your lice? Even from a fence on the rue de la Récolte, it's at least ten thousand for a pistol.'

'A pistol doesn't necessarily kill. Brass knuckles, a switch blade, or a cobbler's awl will do.'

'Stop showing off or I'll throw you under a car!'

'Oh, you don't believe me, do you?'

'No, I don't believe you. Looking as you do, no one will ever believe you, even if you say you're strong enough to squash a bug. Now, so long, little tick!'

Without hesitation he followed me as I went down the street, and he didn't leave me until the day the police started harassing me. I found him a straw mattress and a piece of old tarpaulin as well as a fairly dry place in the market sheds. A few days later he unpacked his bundle. That idiot did have a gun! Later on we used it to rob the Impala Café. He aimed the gun at the barman while I took care of the cash register. I don't know what kind of look there was in his eyes at that moment because we were both masked, but by the way his two little hands gripped the gun, I knew he wouldn't have hesitated to pull the trigger. Poor Sembé! I'm the one who had suggested he go see Mukazano the Madwoman, since no woman would have him. The guy was sweet but ugly! With Mukazano, however, it had to work. She was so out of her head, she did it with anyone without even realizing it: drunks, porters, passing truck drivers. And to think I thought I was making poor Sembé happy!

While she continued to ramble, I tried to imagine his corpse but couldn't. She had reached the touching verse about HIV positive kids, then the part about women victims of rape and, one thing leading to another, to Christ's martyrdom, to the unjust treatment of the infirm, and to the doleful loneliness of the gorillas on Mount Karisimbi. Phew! She adjusted her scarf, rearranged her numerous bracelets, and zipped up her purse, all gestures that, since I've known her, meant she was about to leave. She let out a long sigh and stood up.

'There'll never be enough magistrates on earth to judge all these people! I can't do anything until your file has reached the judge's office. But I spoke with the warden, and he promised to watch over you. I gave him ten thousand for your minor expenses. I'll be back, I don't know when. . . . In two weeks, a month maybe.'

To me it sounded like a fairy tale, and yet it all came true. After that, I could buy cigarettes, glue, bread, and soap. I could even get some porno magazines that this fellow we called Big Man in the condemned wing rented for two cents with the complicity of the jabirus. The life of a nabob compared to the Juniors' Club masses! But that wasn't all. The warden himself came to induct me into my new status. He ordered Ayirwanda to see that I wasn't messed with and that I stayed healthy or risk ending his days in the basement that served as a dungeon. That's how I was spared the slop pail duty and gained the respect of my peers as well as an extra large ladleful of beans during the single meal served in the afternoon.

Does that mean I need to thank her? Certainly not! If she's doing this, she has her reasons. I didn't ask her for anything. . . . And if, milady, I had a complaint, it would be, I assure you, of a very different nature! . . . When she left, she had kissed me not paying any attention to my smell. As if the jabirus had guessed, they let me watch her leave before jostling me back to my quarters. Her breasts were larger, more worthy of being fondled and nibbled than the last time. She wore a flesh-colored wrapper that blended in with her complexion and was so tight around her rump that each time she took a step it looked like she was nude and that it was the skin of her august buttocks quivering before me.[7] For the first time I realized that it had been three years.

Three years since my last lay.

*　*

After fleeing my village, Nyamata, I expected to reach the Byumba caves (where I'd find my parents), when I met up with Funga the witch doctor under a flame tree. But I didn't have the strength to go on. In truth, I didn't even see the need. Would my parents still be in this faraway land of Byumba? That seemed less and less likely in view of the speed at which the world appeared to be moving. I could see refugees marching through the hibiscus and the banana trees. In the hills to the east the sound of cannon fire was becoming more

---

7. *Pagne* in French; a wrapper is a long piece of printed cloth that a woman wraps, rather like a sari, around her body. – Trans.

intense, more frequent. Yet people weren't walking any faster. They were going at the same pace, gripped by the same icy silence that is the rule during prayers and processions. They were walking as if they were returning from a difficult day of labor – or as if they were on their way to God's venerable court for that last judgment Father Manolo was so good at using to make us tremble in the church pews – without looking back and without saying a word to me. While I dozed, a convoy would disappear into the bracken and the heather by the pond, and I'd wake up as another one would come out of the sisal and sorghum fields. I had the feeling the hills were also advancing and the pebbles and the trees were moving by themselves. I laughed briefly thinking about the story our soccer coach used to tell us about the drunk who waits on the sidewalk for his house to come to him. So that nice town of Byumba should be arriving any moment, unless it's already in Burundi!

Before we left, Funga had stuffed a fistful of groundnuts in my pocket. But who's to say if that's what helped me survive the week or weeks that followed. It could just as well have been the effect of my involuntary dozing or my momentary comas as it could have been the mounds of chicken drumsticks and baked bananas appearing in my dreams. Father Manolo was right: 'You idiots shouldn't believe that God keeps you alive for your own pleasure! He's as likely to call you to Him while you're brimming with happiness and health as He is to force you to live amid burning coals. It depends on His own pleasure!'

Then one day my thoughts became clearer and my expression less dazed. I felt a presence; perhaps it was a runaway calf, a daring Gambian rat, or even a shrew. A boy, not much taller than I, dressed like a soldier, was pointing his machine gun at me. He was a RPF![8]

'Well, about time! Who knows how long we've been waiting for your arrival! Thanks anyway for coming to rescue us!'

He kicked me in the ribs and began to address me in a calm, almost soft voice but articulating so I'd understand he wasn't in a mood to argue.

'You'll have to shut up, *génocidaire*! I'm the only one allowed to talk! You'll speak only to answer my questions. Get up! Empty your pockets and cross your hands above your head!'

'Yes, sir! Yes!'

8. Rwanda Patriotic Front: the rebel Tutsi army (now in power).

Sir! I had actually called him 'sir'! And I was shaking as I said it. That's proof that nothing is certain in this damn world! I thought I had used up my stock of timidity and fright. Well, no, fright (and unfortunately greed as well) will always be with human beings as long as they haven't passed through the hands of the undertaker. He threw his pack at me and took on a more menacing look.

'Carry that on your head and start walking, and no scratching and no looking anywhere but where you set your foot!'

Nothing indicated that he could beat me in a fight. Though he was taller than me, my biceps and my hips were more solid. We seemed to be the same age. Nevertheless I obeyed his orders. Oh, if my father had seen me. He'd always reminded me that the two most shameful things that could happen to a young man my age were to pee in bed and to have his actions dictated by one of his peers! 'Don't let the sharp tongues tell you the milk of your mother is not as good as that of others! Understand?' he'd growl when my bravery would begin to wane during a wrestling match. The machine gun pointed at my back didn't explain everything. This young boy was my superior in every way. He was more mature than I. The way he examined the wounded dying in the ditches and the rotting corpses that paddled in the rice fields led me to believe I was dealing with a big brother, even if we had been born on the same day. Life had taught him more than it had taught me. He was beardless like me, but his soul had more hair. My father's famous words came back to me: 'Beards aren't everything, you know! If that was the case, then the billy goat would be the wisest one in the village!' During two days' march, I didn't see him sigh, eat, or drink. Whereas he had let me quench my thirst at the springs and stuff myself with wild fruits! The night of the second day we camped near a stream. He started a fire, grilled some corn, and threw me half. Sitting on a rock he slowly ate his share. Seeing him so at ease, so relaxed, almost vulnerable, I felt a little familiarity was permitted.

'You don't eat much, chief! That's not good when you're still young. My father, Théoneste, used to say: "Eat grasshoppers, eat lizards, eat frogs, just eat! It's in the taste of food that God's spirit can be found." '

'You and I, we signed a pact: I ask the questions first and then you speak!'

'Oh come now, we know each other. . . . well, almost . . . I'm not saying that we've become friends, but . . .'

'I haven't asked any questions yet!'

To keep busy, I tossed a few pebbles into the stream. He lay his weapon down and took a radio out of the side-pocket of his fatigues and began fiddling with it with such concentration I could have thrown his machine gun in the water and run off into the bracken. But what for? For once I had company! Vigilant and faithful besides! And furthermore, all things considered, he'd have caught up with me and coldly beat me or strangled me with his bootlaces. It was glaringly evident that this guy knew what he wanted and was ready to do anything to attain his goal.

'Ask me a question, then. I'm not used to being with people without saying something; that would drive me crazy.'

'Try talking inside your head. You'll see, it'll make you feel better. That's what the captain taught us when we were training in the mountains.'

The radio began to crackle.

'Hello! Captain?' he asked. 'I'm at the stream, and there's no one.'

'Go toward Rutongo; we've taken over the police station. Be here at dawn. The night should be enough time for you to reach the post. Over!'

'Yes, captain! We'll be there by dawn; I'm bringing a package.'

'The name?'

'I haven't grilled him yet. I thought it might be better if you did it yourself. I suspect he's a *génocidaire*. Otherwise he wouldn't have fled. I found him slumped under a tree in the Bugesera brush, probably abandoned by a group of refugees.'

'Just get here and then we'll see about him. Don't forget, tomorrow at dawn. We're going to make a dash for Kigali. Be careful, there are pockets of FAR resistance near Lake Muhazi. Bypass Kigali and take the road to Gitarama. Over!'

He was carrying a flashlight, but he didn't use it for fear of attracting the attention of isolated FAR elements in the hills and the swamp. Like the mutilated bodies scattered through the brush, the night was thick enough to cut with a knife. Not even a hint of the palest star in the sky. But we had no trouble finding our way. If we could endure the stench of the corpses, the mosquito bites, and the thistles, all we had to do was follow the Akanyaru River. When we spotted the road leading to Ruhengeri, he decided we could take a break. We sat in a grove of acacia shrubs. He opened a can of sardines and offered me a cigarette. I took that as a mark of affection. Of course, three days of living together creates bonds. Nevertheless, I had decided to take him at his word and not speak to him until he had asked me a question. I could well imagine that he was a flesh-and-bones human being capable of speech and reason, as Father Manolo would say.

'So your father's name is Théoneste!' he said, just when I expected it the least.

'Yours too!'

'No, his name is Evergiste.'

'Zaire, Tanzania, Uganda?'

'No, Kenya! I was born in Kenya but I joined up in Uganda last year.'

'You all have a strange way of speaking. It's Kinyarwandan, but it sounds like Swahili and English. You really think I'm a *génocidaire*?'

'Everyone is! Children have killed children, priests have killed priests, women have killed pregnant women, beggars have killed other beggars, and so on. There are no innocents left here.'

'I swear, chief . . .'

'You'll speak to the captain. But I won't believe you even if you can convince me you were just born.'

'What are you going to do with me? Are you going to kill me?'

'We kill those who run away. You haven't run away yet.'

'Let me go, chief. We're not far from Gitarama, and I'm certain my parents are in Gitarama.'

'Don't be naïve! First, if you continue taking advantage of my kindness, my mood could change. Second, the captain knows you're here, so if I show up without you, I'm the one going before a firing squad, and anyway I have no desire to let you go even if you had come out of my mother's belly. Besides, you're better off in our hands. With the FAR you wouldn't stand a chance; you could be taken for a traitor since you waited so long to follow the others, and besides, I don't know if you're aware of it, but you look like a Tutsi.'

He let me pick bananas along the road and offered me another cigarette before we reached the police station in Rutongo. It was still too dark to see the paving stones when we reported to the sentry. He took me to an office, signed some papers, and left me with another chief before I ended up at the barracks. I was taken toward the back of the courtyard. There were two crowded cells, and all around, hundreds of people of various ages. The new chief explained to me that they were proven *génocidaires*. The others could remain free until their cases were cleared up. I was told to sit with some other boys. Some were playing *igisoro*, others doing puzzles. There was laughter and arguments. The world hadn't changed.

I didn't want to sleep anymore because I wanted to play too. Seeing the *igisoro* reminded me of the old days when – how long ago was that? – my mother was still there to feed me beans with rancid butter and when, on Sundays, I served mass in church and scored goals for the Juniors' Group. No doubt in another era! I had grown up and everything had changed except my passion for *igisoro*.

'Next game I challenge the best!'

'What's your wager?' replied the stocky boy with the slashed cheek who wanted to be called Musinkôro.

I hadn't counted on that eventuality. In the village, we didn't bet, unless it was on the admiration of the girls watching us play.

'His fingernails, of course!' someone made it his business to answer in my place.

He certainly was right. I was so destitute that my subconscious didn't even make me rummage through my pockets. That's when I remembered my slingshot. My father, Théoneste, made it for me out of prickly pear wood and the rubber from the old inner tube that my bicycle had rolled on for so long. I was very fond of it, but since this was the season for losses, might as well lose that too; and besides, this time I could get something out of the game.

'I have a slingshot.'

'Let's see!'

He tried it out and said, 'Oh, great. With that I can hunt rabbits and,' he looked around to see if any soldiers were near, 'chase off a tribe of Tutsis. You see this silver bracelet? It's a gift from my fiancée. Well I'm so sure I'm going to beat you that I'm betting it anyway. You seem brave enough but, frankly, not very bright.'

'The one without a brain has a high opinion of his own,' they'd say about Théoneste, my father. This kid had such a weak one that he hadn't even retained this proverb. I had no trouble beating him, and since he would never admit defeat, besides the bracelet I eventually took his BP cap, his harmonica, his pack of cigarettes, and a five-thousand-franc bill he had hidden in the lining of his vest. He threatened to bash my head in and to turn me over to the FAR as a traitor as soon as we were out of there. I replied that he could try bashing my head in right now and if he could, not only would I return what I had taken from him but in addition I would be his servant my whole time here. He called me a worm. I called him a prairie dog. We exchanged several blows before the jabirus grabbed us. For two days we had to stay in the famous cells to teach us a lesson. It worked. When we came out, we were both so overcome by heat, hunger, and the brutality of the prisoners that we became friends.

The next day I was summoned to the office. I thought I'd see the one who had brought me here. There were four other young soldiers and someone who appeared to be the famous captain shouting in a telephone. I was told to sit on the floor while he finished his call. When it was over, he motioned to me with his finger, the way we do with puppies.

'Come closer, young man! Sit in this chair; we're going to chat a little.'

He was absent-mindedly leafing through a school notebook. Suddenly he stopped, grabbed a ballpoint pen, and stared into my eyes with his own tiny red ones rimmed with thick eyelashes and deep circles.

'Now you, all we know about you up to now is the name of your father! Didn't you also have a mother?'

'Yes,' I replied as seriously as if he had asked me, Have you also had the whooping cough or scarlet fever? 'Her name is Axelle.'

'Do you know what happened to your parents?'

'They're in Gitarama.'

'Two days ago you were saying Byumba and even, I think, Kayonza. Did they think to give you a name when you came into this world?'

'Yes, Captain! Faustin! Faustin Nsenghimana!'

'Where were you born, Faustin Nsenghimana?'

'Nyamata, in the province of Bugesera!'

'Did you grow up there? Did you learn to shoot pigeons there? Did you go to school there?'

'Yes, Captain!'

'Now, listen carefully and think before you answer: tell me where you were between the seventh and the fifteenth.'

He didn't have to specify the month of April. That's the way everyone refers to this period. 'On the eighth they rounded us up in front of the police station and on the twelfth the Interharamwe arrived,' was commonly heard.[9] Unfortunately President Habyarimana's plane was shot down on the sixth and not the first. It just takes a date to change the course of history. He thought I had misunderstood his question. But, of course, I had understood. I just didn't know where to begin.

'Do you remember April 6?'

'Yes!'

'Then you must also remember the seventh!'

Was it to save my skin, or was it the effect of his authoritative presence? I made a superhuman effort to go back over the famous *advents* that my memory refused to revisit. Suddenly, it was all clear. My mouth opened and words spurted out; he stopped me and had my old road companion join us.

'Find a sheltered corner where he can sleep and see that he has something to drink and eat, as much as he wants. Take a tape recorder and record everything this young man says to you.'

My confession lasted a week. The chiefs got interested in my lowly person. The whole camp was talking about me. Amid the bustle of the soldiers and the officers, there was always a friendly voice to draw me from my reveries.

'Here, Faustin, have a cracker! . . . Don't stay here, Faustin, come listen to this game! In your opinion, who'll win the Afrique des Nations cup, Cameroon or Egypt?'

I was put in charge of the cattle herd the captain had rounded up for the company's ration. Peace was returning to Rutongo. The sound of cannon fire and the parade of refugees had ceased. With the carbine the captain lent me, I could now go as far as the savanna to hunt hares and gazelles. In the evening the men who had spent the day at the operations front were very happy to see some game meat on their plates next to their manioc paste. I had found a new family. There's nothing I'd have liked better than to end my days there. But one day at dawn I was awakened by voices. I went to the barracks entrance and through the gray dawn I could make out some vague shapes singing or shooting guns in the air. Everywhere you could hear: 'Kigali has fallen! Kigali has fallen!'

On the road again, this time behind RPF tanks. Destination, Kigali. The captain gave me a pair of boots, a wool blanket, and a military cap. I had no trouble peddling the blanket and the boots on avenue

9. Hutu militias at the root of the genocide.

du Commerce. I kept the cap to cover the scars on my head. In Kigali, a little pocket money is much better protection than old Funga's charms.

★ ★

Even the fiercest blaze eventually goes out. The sounds of gunfire that had faded in the city also ceased on Mount Kigali. The rattle of the dying and the roar of the tanks gave way to the voices of the women selling papayas and passionfruit. We didn't notice the change. It was as slow and discreet as a young bride entering the marriage hut. Still, it had come, really come. It was everywhere. Even in the stench of the gutters where, as the days went by, the piss of the drunkards and the whores replaced the coagulated blood and the sticky brain matter of the dead. Don't ask me how many months had gone by! Time had been put on the scrap heap like an old wreck. No one would have thought to count it or rearrange it. Night resembled day. Knowing if it was the Tuesday before Lent or Pentecost Monday was useless. Beggars or pencil pushers, we all wanted to hole up somewhere and find a few tubers to gnaw on when, triggered by hunger, a bitter taste of bile would rise to our mouths. And then, slowly, the mind once more began to notice storms and the sound of automobiles, faces, and conversations.

At first, to pass the time, I did what everyone else was doing; I helped the soldiers load up machetes and corpses, direct ambulances toward the wounded who still had a small chance. On his veranda the Greek stored stacks of coffee sacks the whites had neglected to hide in their flight to Kenya. There wasn't a more comfortable bed! Then, when I finished walking around the market along with the widows and the stray dogs, I'd come sleep on top of the sacks. I'd see lots of kids my age, but I didn't speak to them. What for? I suppose that, like me, they didn't feel the need to trust or to play. For food I'd climb over the market wall and with a broken spade dig up remnants of groundnuts, manioc, and green bananas left in the mud. Simple! When panic takes over a city, the first things people abandon are bars, dance clubs, brothels, and the markets. So when famine began to prowl, I had my own personal field ripe for the plowing. It's incredible the amount of treasures people leave behind on the ground! I'd easily collect a bag of groundnuts, a bunch of manioc, and a pot of bananas every day and, one time, even a bowl of smoked fish hidden under a stall. I'd wash these precious foodstuffs in a puddle of water, start a fire on a trash pile on rue de l'Epargne, and voilà! I wouldn't say that my life was as good as at the camp in Rutongo, but I couldn't complain. I had managed to rescue something out of the chaos. And then, since we're never sure which way things will go, I had learned quite well to make do with the way things were.

Until the day when from the Greek's veranda I saw a policeman throw open the market gate and civilians in cars invade the streets. Old Funga is right: 'Life marches on, but often in the wrong direction.' During wartime, I could eat for free. During peacetime, I had to work really hard to earn my meager fare. Early in the morning I'd hire myself out to unload bundles for the fabric vendors and kegs for the banana-beer vendors. During the day I'd stand in front of the Caritas Bookstore to watch over cars. With the coins I earned, I could buy manioc paste and green sauce from the women cooking on the sidewalks. One evening as I was enjoying one of these delicious dishes, I felt someone brush against my back and saw a hand slip under my arm and steal my plate. I turned around. A boy was standing behind me.

'Where did you steal this plate of manioc? And don't tell me you sold your slingshot so you could eat!'

It was Musinkôro. He placed the plate on the bench and hugged me the way a brother would have.

'So, you're still alive! Like me and like Msîri! But you don't know Msîri! I'll introduce you to him one day.'

'Musinkôro! Musinkôro!'

All I could say was that name. Incredible. It wasn't just the game of *igisoro*, my slingshot, and his harmonica that linked us, it was a whole bloodline. Thunder rumbled a dozen times a day. The rain came rushing down the slopes with the speed of Kagera Falls and washed away the last traces of dust and blood. My father, Théoneste, loved this splendid time of year above all others. He was convinced that *itumba* (that's how we called the rainy season in our language, Kinyarwanda) hadn't been planned by the gods just to wash the earth and water the plants. It played a major role in cleansing hearts and renewing ties among men. That must have been the case: *itumba* had purified my soul and Musinkôro's and reunited us in the heat of a new blood relationship. This called for a celebration. He took me to the Eden

Bar. The owner didn't like us to hang around. But Musinkôro knew the waitress, Scholastique. He motioned to her and she discreetly brought us our beers on the sidewalk. What better place in the world to get sloshed than the garbage dump on rue des Coopératives! That's where we went to drink. After that, we began to sing as fervently as a bunch of peasants drinking banana beer to celebrate the harvest. Singing is done with our whole God-given body; talking is done with the mouth only. It's better this way – to sing and not talk.

The Greek, too, returned to assess the damages: broken windows, decimated chickens, and coffee sacks ripped open. I had acquired the habit of sleeping wherever sleep overtook me, at the foot of the war memorial, at the entrance of the post office, or in the area of rue Lac-Rweru. I was thinking of taking my friend there. But, as if he had guessed my intentions, he suddenly asked me, 'Do you know about HQ?'

'I have nothing against soldiers, but if I can help it, I'd rather avoid them.'

'You don't get it, Faustin Nsenghimana! I'm not talking about the barracks. I'm talking about my home – our home – I almost forgot my little family. So come on!'

The famous HQ was located in a no man's land isolated between the shantytowns of Muhima and Boulevard Nyabugogo. What a godsend! While in the town overrun by soldiers and refugees – people were sleeping fifteen to a room – he had found this. An abandoned but still new building overrun by grass so tall it was invisible from the street. Brand new, that is, unfinished! The doors hadn't been hung and the front steps were just begun. The floors were spiked with sharp stones (the builders hadn't had time to pound). Luckily, there had been time to finish the structure. And Musinkôro, who thought of everything, had laid out cardboard boxes, jute sacks, bits of sheet metal, and split barrels for protection from the rain. Here too, the government had made plans for a school, a health unit, or a neighborhood center, and as often happens, the money had disappeared. Some twenty kids of both sexes were living here. At first glance some didn't seem to be more than ten years old. When we arrived, the little clan stopped its yelling and squabbling. They all dropped their rag balls and their cardboard rattles and went to their corners. It reminded me of when the teacher walks into the classroom. And Musinkôro actually looked like a schoolteacher or the head of a family, not like a gang leader.

He sat on an empty drum lying about, carefully removed his sneakers without laces, soiled with creosote and tar, then said for all to hear.

'So, what about today?'

'Canisius picked up a billfold and the girls brought back rice and some mutton from the Muslim district. They were handing them out to all the believers passing by. It's Eid al-Adha!'[10]

'This billfold, where'd you pick it up?' asked Musinkôro in a suspicious tone that made everyone laugh.

'In front of the Mille Collines Hotel, I swear!' replied the one called Canisius.

'Canisius, you're even less believable when you swear! Wasn't it in the glove compartment of an NGO car instead?[11] Oh, those poor whites, they come here to help us get civilized, and all we do is pick their pockets. All right, let's see it!'

'Threw it away!'

'Oh!'

'Because of the papers! The cops, they never believe you when you tell them you just picked something up.'

'How much?'

'Fifty thousand . . . Or so. I ate some kebabs at Célestine's and I bought a pair of shoes. I've been going barefoot for so long my feet are full of ticks and broken glass.'

'I'm not accusing you of anything, Canisius! . . . Actually, yes, of swearing when you don't need to. Where are the spoils of war?'

'Under the avocado tree!'

Strewn about the largest room were a chipped stove, some old Guigoz milk bottles, some bowls, some pots, and so on.

Musinkôro led me to it.

'Let's taste the pious Muslims' mutton! Let's eat what God gives us today. Who's to say if we'll have a tomorrow? You see, here, we're safe. No one knows we exist, neither the cops nor the neighbors. But the eyes of an informer can show up any time. Then it's jail for us all. At best, eviction after a thorough search leaving us without even our fingernails to scratch our butts.'

Out of who knows where, he brought out a jerry can full of banana

10. The Islamic Feast of Sacrifice that commemorates the willingness of Abraham to sacrifice his son at God's request. – Trans.

11. Nongovernmental organization. – Trans.

beer. He summoned the others. We were forming a large circle around a dish when suddenly there was a strange noise among the corn and the banana trees. It sounded like a chase or a boar defending its babies. The sound of footsteps echoed in the courtyard then and on the poorly joined steps of the front entrance. A boy holding a bloody knife in his hand burst into the room where we were eating. Gasping, full of sweat, he leaned against the wall to catch his breath. We were so surprised, all we could do was stare speechlessly. Finally, he coughed lightly and words poured out of his mouth in spurts, as if they were burning his tongue.

'Boulevard Nyabugogo . . . in front of the Welcome Hotel . . . I had to stab the palm of his hand. . . . He didn't want to let go of his camera, the moron!'

He took off his jacket. Underneath he had a brand new Kodak slung over his shoulder. Musinkôro was shaken by endless laughter.

'Faustin,' he said, 'let me introduce you to Msîri. I told you about Msîri, didn't I?'

That's how I ended up at HQ. The nights are cool in my country, and Musinkôro remembered to give me a sheet of tarpaulin. As a precaution the girls slept in the room farthest from the entrance, and us boys would spread out at will in the large room on the left where it wasn't so damp. We called the house the HQ because we hadn't come up with another name. In reality, we went there just to sleep. During the day, there would have been plenty of curious onlookers to spot us. We'd get up when the cock crowed and hit the streets in groups of two or three. The girls, around the hotels, Musinkôro, on rue du Commerce, Msîri, near the banks, the others, between the artisans' stalls and the war memorial, my team and I, in front of the Caritas Bookstore. Occupying these locations meant the whole town was covered. No one was forced to remain at the assigned spot. On the contrary, Musinkôro urged us to act with the greatest mobility. My territory was comprised of the best parking lots between rue du Lac-Buera (the one the Caritas Bookstore is on) and place de la Constitution to the north, avenue des Grands-Lacs on the other side. Our role was to watch the cars of the big shots and the beautiful ladies. Ezechiel, who had no equal in opening car doors, would help me give oil refills or wipe windshields. I'd let him rifle through the trunks and the glove compartments. If he found some little thing of interest, he'd start singing and Tatien or Ephrem would appear from the crowd of passersby hanging around the market, grab the thing, and get rid of it farther away at a prearranged location, like behind a fence, in a banana grove, under the rubbles of a hut, or wherever. Canisius's job was to be on the move. He'd go from one group to the other checking that everything was going smoothly. The girls were supposed to look pitiful enough to move the rich pedestrians yet dressed in clean enough outfits that, if the opportunity presented itself, they could slip between the sheets of some lecher loaded with dough. And the boys, besides their jobs as shoeshines or porters, were supposed to stash in hiding places all the food or jewelry they could pinch without getting caught. At night the oldest would make the rounds of the hiding places, and we'd bury our loot in a hole we'd dug under the avocado tree. The girls would cook while we'd entertain each other with jokes and smoke grass or sniff glue. Josepha, Gabrielle, Alphonsine, and Emilienne were the prettiest. I'd screw one or another while everyone else was asleep or sometimes at the market when we'd stay a little longer to pick up a few more coins. Those were happy times, among the best of my life. In fact I rarely thought about my parents. It was an ordinary life, fulfilled and orderly, and it distracted us from thoughts of the past or the future. Although – of course – nothing is perfect. We also had our own little problems like sickness, floods, and a few little rows over a bit of coke or a chick's ass; they would result in either a black eye or a slashed cheek. I must admit, work didn't always go without incidents. For example, that day when a customer accused me of stealing his car radio. That moron Canisius! I had told him a thousand times not to touch the car radios or the jewelry, to stick to the practical, the discreet, the useful (money, clothes, food, and at the outside calculators or cameras, those were good!).

The guy grabbed both my ears and lifted me so high that my feet were level with his chest.

'This kid stole my car radio! . . . You know what I'm going to do, huh? Burn your thieving hands and then drag you to the police station! That way no one else will have to endure what I did.'

He was pounding my forehead with his large hands and punching my stomach with his knees. Onlookers were coming out of every-where and had surrounded us. But it was to enjoy the show, not because of my cries for help. Luckily, a young woman got out of a car, made her way through the crowd lambasting those who were laughing at my troubles and freed me from the situation. It was she: Claudine!

I was so worn out and terrorized that I let out a fart and relieved myself of a few gallons of pee in the ditch.

'Why don't you shit too, thief!' someone yelled out. 'If it had been up to me, you wouldn't have a face anymore! Parasite! Nobody!'

'Be quiet, all of you!' the young woman shouted.

She walked up to my tormentor and looked him in the eyes.

'You have no right to hit him! Besides, what proof is there that he stole it? Aren't you ashamed of yourself, a boy barely twelve?'

I took the occasion to pound the nail in: 'I've been watching cars here for three months! Who's ever seen me steal anything? It's because I'm little, right? Yeah, that's it! If I were as strong as you, you'd never have dared!'

I sat down on an old wheel lying about. I really didn't feel like crying but I hid my face in my shirttail, rubbed saliva over my eyes and let out the most pitiful cries of distress I could muster. That did the trick. She came near me, patted my head and comforted me with words that could have only come from the mouth of a mistress. 'No doubt,' I thought, 'she's going to give me some money and ask me to sleep with her.'

The incident over, the passersby scattered toward rue du Commerce and avenue de la République to sell their soaps and their candles and go back to their currency and drug trafficking. She helped me stand up and led me toward the ice-cream vendor's cart. She bought me a vanilla cone, cookies, and gave me some money.

'Tell me, where do you come from, young man? From Cyangungu Province or Ruhengeri?'

'No, Kigali!'

'And where are your parents?'

'Here in Kigali! Our house is in Gikondo!'

'It was your parents who told you to come here and watch cars?'

'No, it was my choice. They don't know anything about it.'

She looked at me as if I had just dropped from the moon. I didn't care that it was hard for her to believe me because I enjoyed talking like this. So I shamelessly went on in the same vein.

'I'm doing it so I can afford to go to the movies and buy a pair of sneakers and a nice football.'

She was pensive for a moment, then she looked up toward the sky. Perhaps the outcome of my case was to be found there.

'Tell me, young man, what's your name?'

'Cyrille! Cyrille Elyangashu! In Gikondo everyone knows the Elyangashu family!'

'Well, Cyrille, from now on you're going to watch my car. My name is Claudine. Claudine Karemera! This turned out to be a lucky day for you, you made a new friend.'

I returned to HQ in good spirits. That night, I didn't feel the stones under my ribs. I slept without thinking about Gabrielle, Emilienne, or Josepha.

I was in love!

★   ★

How come I hadn't met Claudine sooner? Her office was just a step away. She was accustomed to parking on rue de l'Epargne so her car could be in the shade. Now it was different. She'd drive right up to me and let me guide her to the space cluttered with bricks I had reserved for her. We'd reached the point where she didn't have to pay me anymore. I was proud when she'd kiss me as she got out of her car. She always had candies with her, and when she opened her wallet, she didn't hand me coins but real bills. That happened once, sometimes twice a week.

'Cyrille,' she'd say, 'tonight I have a meeting that might go on for a long time. Can you watch it anyway?'

Of course I could! For her, it was a real pleasure. The nightmare was the others with their big four-wheel-drive vehicles and their bags; they'd park any which way and scold you as they handed you a coin. Some never gave anything. 'Today, kid, boss has no change! Tomorrow!' She was different. She didn't come just to get rid of her car, she also came for me. It was a date. The subject had never been brought up, but by coincidence, she'd wear the perfume that deep down inside I wished her to wear. At night, if I dreamed of her in a suit, it was the very suit she'd have on the next day; or in a wrapper and it was the wrapper that flared as she got out of her car, revealing a knee and a thigh. Obviously I'd have preferred it if she didn't kiss my hair but instead would decide to touch me where my desire was aroused.

Then one day, things took a bad turn. I waited in vain. That put me in a bad mood. I had an argument with the ice-cream vendor and didn't buy the bank guard his usual soda at the market. She showed up late in the afternoon with a look on her face that I didn't like at all.

'Get in!' she told me as soon as she was parked.

I got in. Right away it was the question I had been dreading.

'So where do I drop you off, Cyrille? But is it Cyrille or Faustin?'

'My name is Cyrille. Drop me off outside of Gikondo.'

'I did a thorough search of Gikondo. I even checked the court records. There's not a single Elyangashu there. Elyangashu, are you sure that's a name from around here? You didn't invent it?'

I didn't have the strength to answer. At Constitution Square, she turned left, went past the central traffic circle, drove onto Boulevard Nyabugogo.

'But! . . .'

'But what, Faustin?'

'Where are we going? Gikondo is the other way!'

'I can't wait to see this famous HQ,' she hissed in an ironic tone that made me want to throw her to the pavement. 'Tatien told me everything, kid. He was even kind enough to introduce me to Musinkôro, Msîri, Gabrielle, and the others. I thought you were a nice boy, but no, you're the most secretive of all!'

'We don't need anyone. I certainly don't!'

' "He who thinks he can do without others will die!" You see, I'm not just fluent in Kinyarwanda, I know its proverbs too.'

'I'm not the worst off. I still have my legs, my arms. My ears are intact, and my eyes are still where they belong! There must still be widows and orphans! There are plenty of shelters in this country. Why don't you help them?'

'We'll see if HQ is a palace or a sordid shelter!'

For her visit Musinkôro had the mats and the foam mattresses, all the old rags and the bowls put away. So I was swimming in conspiracy. She visited the premises without paying attention to me. She reminded me of the assistant to the mayor in Nyamata when he inaugurated a new health clinic. She sat in the metal chair and accepted a baked banana. I never wanted to see her, feel her, or listen to her again. How frivolous! She was touching Canisius's cheeks; taking Tatien by the shoulder, Josepha by the hands; she was asking

Emilienne how long she'd had her cough, if she wasn't afraid of the rain, the rats, the mosquitoes, the weirdos prowling around. That was making me yawn. I wanted to scratch her and, once my fit of jealousy was over, to throw her down right there in front of everyone and wallow in her body. She brought her hands up to her hair to fix a few strands, then, as if she had just noticed my presence, stared at me with her luminous eyes.

'I know that your parents are in Kibuyé. But the rest of you? Do you still have your parents?'

Thank goodness Sembé was there to snub her a little.

'Big sister, there you are quietly sitting in your hut. Lightning hits your roof. Are you going to remember to take your parents as you flee?'

'No!'

'Well!'

'How long ago did lightning strike? Six months, nine months, a year! That's plenty of time to find out who's dead, who's not, who was able to flee, and who's in jail!'

'This time it was not just lightning but all the lightning in the world!' Sembé replied in a fouler mood than usual.

'That doesn't give you the right to isolate yourselves! If you don't need others, others need you. Isolation, that's the source of our woes. Here, everyone withdraws on a hill as if the neighbors had eyes in the middle of their foreheads. . . . Take that any way you wish, but I don't have the right to leave you alone! I might as well tell you now, we're going to see each other again.'

That made me sit up.

'You don't mean that you're going to come back?' I said worriedly.

'Yes I do!'

'Here?'

'Here! No one's going to know. I'm not a cop, and I'm not an informer.'

And so she came back! She didn't just return with her mother hen ways and her sexy rump that drove me wild. She also brought aspirins, ointments, compresses, jams . . . the sort of stuff you see in the hands of priests and nurses. Now that she had met my buddies, I thought I'd become a man like others for her, an Ezechiel, a Canisius, any old poor Seth or Deogratias wandering between Lake Muhazi and

Mount Kigali. So I was particularly flattered when she turned toward me and said, 'The folding bed, that's for you!'

It was the following month, I believe, that she introduced us to that white woman we'd end up calling Miss Human Rights, or just simply 'the Hirish woman.' Our language, Kinyarwanda, had not anticipated sounds to pronounce a name as implausible as Una Flannery O'Flaherty. Thank goodness Canisius, who was born near the Tanzanian border, spoke some English. On her four-wheel-drive vehicle there wasn't HCR but Human Rights Watch, a thing that Canisius tried to explain to us with little success. Already we weren't exactly thrilled about Sister Claudine's visits (she loved it when we called her that), so you can imagine a white woman! We hadn't consulted each other, and none of us had made any special effort to take on a hostile attitude, but it was so evident that Claudine was embarrassed.

'She's neither Belgian nor French. She's Irish. Have you heard of the Irish?'

'No!'

'Then that proves they haven't harmed us. So, come on, give Una a friendly greeting!'

Since nothing was happening, the said Una approached us revealing her strong white teeth all impeccably aligned. She knelt in front of young Alphonsine.

'Don't worry, Claudine, it's because we don't know each other yet. But we will soon, right?'

The ice still wasn't broken. She didn't lose her composure for all that.

'Wait,' she said.

And she disappeared toward her vehicle parked in the grass. She came back with hoops, balls, dolls, whistles. Everyone ran up to the providential greasy pole to grab an object, stick it under an arm, and go back to their places with the same sullen look as before. Once again Claudine had to come to the rescue.

'Isn't it nice what she just did? Say 'thank you' at least!'

Una slapped her furrowed brow; she had a new idea.

'Oh, I bet you all love music! Rap! Soukouss![12] Salsa! You know what

12. Music from the Congo, the most popular music in much of Africa during the 1990s. – Trans.

we're going to do Saturday? We're going to organize a little party. I'll come with my tape player. You'll come too, won't you, Claudine?'

They came with plenty of cookies, sodas, and passionfruit juice. Musinkôro, who was quite ingenious, had remembered to stash some glue and beer near the avocado tree and so, pretending to go pee, we'd take turns going to it to renew our vitality.

I'm not saying she wasn't nice, Miss Human Rights. But her country was unknown under our sun, and frankly, we were better off without her.

⋆ ⋆

One night, as she was leaving her office, Claudine did something totally uncustomary. She took me to the Eden Café for a drink.

'I spoke to Una about you. She's agreed to take you with her.'

'Take me where?'

'Wait! Una came to Rwanda to open an orphanage on the road to Rwamagama. It's now ready. There's water, electricity, even an infirmary. The orphanage opened three months ago. As you can imagine, it's already full. But I really insisted, so she finally agreed to make room for you. You're moving in next week. What do you think?'

'I can't say I don't dream of sleeping in a real house. But this . . .'

'Una is an angel. Also, think of your health! You'll end up getting gangrene or a hernia sleeping in the rain. I'm already worried about your cough; there's pus in your ears and a rash that worries me.'

'I don't want to go without the others.'

'The others will go too, when there's room.'

Without realizing it I had just signed a contract. That was it, the City of Blue Angels. I moved in reluctantly; in fact it was with the secret hope that I'd see Claudine's ass more often. I was stripped of my rags, deloused, my head, armpits, and pubes, shaved; I was taken to a disinfecting room and given new clothes. It was a large dormitory in the shape of an airplane: one wing for the boys and another for the girls. We were lodged eight to a room. We slept on bunk beds under clean blue sheets and wool blankets. We were given aspirins and enough to eat. There was a little two-room school at the foot of the hill and a playing field in front of the covered playground. The City of Blue Angels had only two drawbacks: strict discipline (but Claudine had warned me about that) and the absolutely unbearable hysterical weeping off and on, day or night, coming from the girls' wing. During the day, I'd go far out toward the manioc fields to lessen its effect on my head, and at night, even though I stuck castor beans in my ears, I couldn't sleep. The cries were so intense they scared us more than the bursts of thunder coming from the bowels of the tin mine next door. No one could ignore them. We started to call them 'the alarm bell.' It was so bad the teacher would interrupt her lesson and the washerwomen on their way back from the well would stop under the jacarandas until 'the alarm bell' was silent. Who could possibly be emitting such inhuman cries? I asked boarders and cooks. But no one could satisfy my curiosity. Some talked of madness and a curse. According to those who had seen them, there were three (three girls, or else two girls and a boy, depending on the person's eyesight). They had been wandering through the brush among the wild cats and the monkeys when an old priest found them. They were in such a state of hysteria and malnutrition that they had to be bottle-fed and then they were locked in a windowless room for fear they would break the panes, for fear they would set fire to the dormitories, for fear they would eat the Hirish woman alive. Isolating them was a wise decision. They had been here a year and they never set foot in the halls, had never discovered the vegetable garden or tried to play on the swings! A privileged few had caught glimpses of them when their door was opened a crack to go in and loosen their straight jackets and to force them to swallow two or three spoonfuls of soup. Only the Hirish woman and the nurse could have described them (their facial features, the shape of their ears, in case they were still whole). But our good Hirish woman was as silent as a confessor, and the nurse, well, outside of quinine and bandages, she never had much to say.

The director asked to meet me. He was waiting in his office and he wasn't alone. The Hirish woman was next to him, knitting. Seeing the attention with which she watched me enter, I figured that she was the one who had sent for me, even if it meant letting my fellow countryman sound me out (as manioc eaters, of course we could understand each other better). They both wore an expressly serious look. Now really, they weren't going to accuse me of breaking into the store to steal that famous box of corned beef, since Hillaire, the night watchman, had been exposed and sacked! In any case, the affair seemed serious. The proof is Miss Human Rights didn't ask me as she usually did when she'd meet me in the workshop or the dining hall: 'So, Faustin, have you heard from Claudine?' How could I have heard from Claudine? I never got letters and never went out except to accompany Bizimungu the driver to pick up a package at the airport or to buy tubers at the market.

'Tell me, Faustin, you're from Nyamata, aren't you?'

'Yes, sir, Director!'

He gave Miss Human Rights a doubtful look, as if to ask if he could continue.

'Hmm, well! . . . And your parents' names are Axelle Kabarungi and Théoneste Nsenghimana, right?'

'There's no doubt about that!'

'Tell us a little bit about Nyamata.'

'Okay. There's the church, the soccer field, the Italian woman's pigsties, the Prudence drugstore, the Shell station, the Oprovia branch, and, of course, city hall.'

'Like everyone else, you hear strange cries here? . . . And of course, you figure those children have gone mad? . . . You see, if we could at least find out where they're from, maybe we can't give them back their sanity, but we might be able to make them less wild.'

'What do I, Faustin Nsenghimna, have to do with all this?'

'On the face of it, nothing! It's just that we're pretty certain they're from your region. When those three little devils start to rant, they say things that sound like Ntarama, Nyamata, Bugesear, Ngenda. All those villages are near each other, if I'm not mistaken?'

'Same pastures, same hospital, same diocese, same weekly market!'

'That means, if our speculations are correct, you could have run across them one day, or someone who resembles them. Now, think carefully. Have you heard words like *chalchiche, kessa, con comme lèche, espera, certo?*'

'That sounds like Italian to me,' said the Hirish woman, speaking up for the first time. 'And if that's confirmed, then they're really from Nyamata. That's the only village where an Italian woman lived, this Antonin. . . .'

'No, Tonia! Tonia Locatelli!' I corrected professorially.

'This Tonia Locatelli who was carved up two years ago almost live on international radio airwaves. Did you know her?'

'Did I know her! Our house was right next to her cowsheds. She gave my sisters reading and embroidery lessons. After the harvest, Father would take care of her pigsties in exchange for a little meat and milk. After one of her trips to Italy, she brought back some medicine for Mother curing her of this numbness she always had in her legs and . . .'

'Excuse me for interrupting. Would it scare you to go see them?'

Miss Human Rights called the nurse who turned up with her whip and her enormous bunch of keys. The children were leaning against the only wall lighted by the outside lamp, but I recognized them without having to open my eyes wide.

⋆   ⋆

They didn't think it was necessary to clap me in irons or to strap me in a straight jacket. Yet they took the precaution to put big old Zizimungu at my bedside. To control my agitation, all he had to do was place his elbow on my spine.

Of course, later on, Hitimana, the one who has the bed above mine, explained to me how I had fainted. 'The nurse used the sprinkler to chase us out of the hall where they had laid you out. But I refused to leave. I hid behind a post waiting for you to croak. You see, I've never seen anyone do it. Always people groaning, bleeding, or shivering yet not dying, even if they held their guts in their hands and had a steel shard in the middle of their skull. Those traitors, they'd always wait until I'd left to decide to give up the ghost! So for once, I thought, there's someone really dying in front of me!'

My fever and my convulsions were abating, and I was alone in the infirmary. Slowly I learned to walk around in the hall and to take my meals in the dining room. And since I was drawing water from the well without throwing it in the dormitories and weeding the vegetable garden without pulling up the tomatoes and the beans, they concluded I hadn't gone mad. That would have really bugged them if I'd croaked or gone round the bend. I had become important, the possessor of a secret, the only one able to solve the mystery of the three little devils, as they said.

But to enlighten them, first I had to start clearing things up for myself. I came out of the coma in a terrible state. I had bruises all over from bumping against the bed rails and the walls. It was as if storms raged inside my head from all the drugs they made me swallow. For several days I had delirium, tirelessly repeating: *chalchiche, kessa, certo,* and so on. Miss Human Rights and the director would take my pulse and watch my lips. 'What? . . . Give it a try! . . . You recognized them, didn't you? Tell us everything!' Slowly the fog in my mind lifted, the words became more precise, the images clearer, more evocative. . . . *Salsiche, queija, risotto, cafe com lette, ciao, certo, arrivederci, muito obrigado, grazie.*

The road from Kigali goes over the Nyabarongo bridge, snakes between the hills, then divides the sorghum fields and the sisal plantations in two. There's the Oprovia branch, the soccer field, the beauty parlor, the courthouse. After the Fraternité Bar, it splits: one segment ventures toward the fern hedges and the little red-dirt houses and merges with the *grévéhia* trees, the papyri, and the fields strewn with manure along the east side of the village; the other turns to gravel and dies out toward the south in a courtyard planted with hibiscus and giant kapok trees.[13] On the left, the church, whose trapeze-shaped roof hides the Brazilian convent; on the right, the Italian woman's house, separated from the cowsheds and the pigsties by a thin reed fence (the hut where we were born is right behind, amid those thorny trees we call *umugnigna*). Straight ahead, the vegetable garden, the priests' houses, the home economics school, the boarding school . . . I can see the Italian woman in her blue overalls, slaving away between the kitchen and the cowsheds, the Brazilian mother superior who's come for her milk, Father Manolo and his breviary, two little girls chewing on a papyrus stalk, and behind them, a bawling pot-bellied little boy who has so much difficulty walking it's as if with each step he takes the good Lord will call him back.

Hitimana takes great pleasure in recounting how, infuriated by their insistence, I broke the director's glasses and hurled the metal chair where they usually kept my phials and my tablets as well as the compresses used to mop up my sweat, and I screamed so loud I could be heard a half-day's march away.

'One of them is named Esther, the other Donatienne! The little boy, that's Ambroise! They're my brother and sisters. My brother and sisters, you idiots.'

---

13. *Grévéhia*: a tree resembling the cypress tree, common in Rwanda. – Trans.

They let me regain my wits before bringing us together (two pairs of lunatics under the same roof don't necessarily a family make!). The first time it was in front of the Hirish woman, the director, and the nurse only. They came to get me out of bed early, well before the baker's delivery van arrived and Célestin, the cook, had filled his jugs with coffee with milk in it. They moved aside to let me go in first. They were standing close to each other behind the doorframe, and they were observing me as if I were a demon. It might as well be my fault! The famine, the cholera, the boiling lava flow in Karisimbi's crater, they were all my fault! I might as well be the one who moved the rock of Kagera, thrust a stake up Mrs. Mukandori's vagina (whose impaled mummy image went round the world), stirred up the demons, and unleashed the elements!

I tripped against an empty bowl, slipped on traces of excrement. The light from the candle the mother superior was holding behind me prevented me from trampling on Ambroise and falling over Donatienne. They were stretched out in scattered rows on the floor, worse off than I had imagined. It was incorrect to say they had lost weight, rather they had shrunk, had gone back to being the children I used to know. I was nine, Esther, seven, Donatienne, four, and Ambroise, two. Father had gone off to work in the mines of Zaire. Mother was hoeing the bean field near the swamp. It was up to me to amuse them with rag dolls and sardine cans filled with pebbles and when necessary give them curdled milk or sorghum gruel.

I stepped forward with a serenity that astonished me. I was near the goal. I was going to be able to embrace them. But the screams! I stepped back toward the door where the others had stayed, and they ceased immediately. This happened two or three times. That's when I remembered the lullaby our mother used to sing to us. Ambroise alone reacted; the others, knowingly averting their bulging and bloodshot eyes, carried on with their horrible wails. I threw my arms wide open as Mother used to when she'd return from the fields with ripe avocados and delicious passionfruit juice. He curled up in a ball like a kitten and began to sob, but finally he let me kiss him. I walked around rocking him, trying my best to imitate Mother's voice and gestures. The sobs became less frequent. He snuggled against my chest and a minute later was sleeping like a log. No doubt contagion spreads; the girls, now quiet, were watching the whole thing with the kind of curiosity I had when there were love scenes on the TV screen at the Fraternité Bar! I stopped humming the lullaby and began to pray to all the powers I could think of: Imana and the Holy Spirit, the rock of Kagera and old Funga's charms. I hoped they'd all pool their miracles together to sustain forever the calm now reigning. I noticed with relief that the two little girls' eyes were no longer on Ambroise's arms wrapped around my neck but were now fixed on my face. I couldn't tell if they had recognized me. But it was comforting to see them yawning and rubbing their eyes as if they had just come out of a gentle sleep. 'The lizard crawls with the lizard and the doe recognizes the doe!' old Funga used to say.

★   ★

They were moved to another room. The administrator was right, my presence had a beneficial effect on them. Though we did have to wait a couple of weeks for them to call me by my name and three for them to acknowledge the existence of our parents. On the other hand, they very quickly stopped soiling their pants and during the first days they began to emit human language sounds. From then on I was allowed to take care of them. I washed them, deloused them, stuffed them with yogurt and sorghum gruel, coconut milk, and passionfruit juice. When they had regained enough flesh to be able to endure the effects of an injection and to reach the hallway on their own two feet, the town doctor was sent for. Four months later, they had become boarders just like the others, taking showers alone and eating in the dining hall without help. Still I wasn't ready to ask what had happened to them from the day we had left each other for fear that their flesh would once more turn to shreds and the racket would start up again. Had I been thinking about them this whole time? I wasn't sure. All my memories had been of our parents, so in a way I had never thought of them without our parents. Watching them in the courtyard or at the school's covered playground, I'd try to remember the last moments we had experienced together. It came to me in a flash that they weren't at the church when Corporal Nyumurowo grabbed my kite. No, they hadn't been forgotten at the stable or in the banana plantation. The morning of the fifteenth, before the trucks entered the town square,

44

the Brazilian mother superior had come as usual to pick up her milk cans. After the Italian woman's death, my father had been in charge of that chore, 'until' as he liked to say. 'Until what, poor Théoneste?' the mother superior would ask, as irritated by the word as by his drinking bouts. 'Well, until they bring another white woman or until I croak!' That had been going on for two years! No new white woman had come, and my old father, Théoneste, was still fit as a fiddle, even on this turbulent morning of the fifteenth when the future seemed so dark that, at around six o'clock, Funga had thrown his books of magic and his potions into the swamp. I remember that the mother superior, who really enjoyed mocking him, had noticed it.

'You don't seem too worried! Of course, to worry one has to have a little bit of smarts. And you, well you don't even know what that is. You're the kind who'd have a good laugh all alone on the gallows and not know what was happening to him. Oh, but you're right after all! It's better than all this agitation. I hear that some people have even fled into the papyrus swamp. Those idiots, I keep telling them nothing's going to happen here! It has always stopped at Kanzenzé; it's never gone beyond the bridge, even in 1972. We're not accustomed to this around here! We prayed all night long at the convent. The Belgian fathers have said a mass. Nothing'll happen, you'll see!'

She said that as my father was helping her houseboy load the cans on the cart, guffawing with that blessed dimwitted laugh of his that he'd had since birth and that reassured all the neighbors. She had almost reached the vegetable garden when she changed her mind, as if she suddenly doubted what she'd just said. 'Bring me the little ones! They'll help me shell beans. And then . . .'

I don't think I remember what she said after that. But at least things were clear: they weren't at the church when Corporal Nyumurowo grabbed my kite, they were at the convent with the Brazilian nuns. That's what saved them. The church's function is not only to save our souls; it's also to save our lives. Mother told me how, when she was a young girl, Father Manolo saved hers inadvertently in 1972. She was getting ready to join her friend Suzanne in Kanzenzé to make pearl belts and those serval-skin skirts we call inkindi, when Farther Manolo reminded her he was counting on her for the choir the next day. And she was right to comply because the next day her friend Suzanne got a surprise visit from a machete whiz.

In any case I was no longer alone in the world. The good Lord had been overly generous with his miracles to allow me to find my brother and my sisters; he could do even better and let me find my parents, anywhere! I just should never listen to people of bad omen. Father is in Mabanza, and Mother is with him. As soon as the rock of Kagera is back in its place, we'll be back home, just in time for the banana harvest and the feast of the *intore*. Once again, Cousin Thaddeus and I will make *igisoro* games, shields, and spears, and during the off-season, when there are no more yams to plant and the sisal has been cut, we'll roughhouse to test our strengths. I'll watch them grow, and a day will come when Esther and Donatienne will marry. Then I'll kill two strong buffaloes, and I'll give them the horns to hang outside their huts. I'll drink like six warriors, I'll dance the dance of the *intore*, and I'll challenge with a spear the husbands of the twelve mistresses I'll have acquired in the meantime.

⋆ ⋆

The food was good at the City of the Blue Angels. We slept well, and we laughed. We didn't have head lice nor those mean toe ticks that tear at your flesh. There was all that was needed to cure diarrhea and wounds, clean your scrapes and your scabies, to protect you from leprosy and 'concosomething.' No, I had no complaints. Was it because of Claudine? In spite of my moodiness, I was in the Hirish woman's good graces. And so Célestin, the cook, would give me a second helping of mashed yams even if I wasn't hungry any more, and when the sun was too hot, the nurse would excuse me from work in the garden so I could help her stock the medications. *Pernangamate* on the right, *merchrome* on the left and *pellicinin* on the middle shelves. She'd perch herself on a footstool to reach her ointments and her compresses. I could see hair showing through her panties. Her thighs were not as firm and were more scraped than Claudine's. I'd have jumped her bones anyway if she'd been willing. Since my arrival I hadn't come within five feet of a woman. At night, I'd rummage under the sheets thinking about Joséphina or Emilienne. I wouldn't have minded it if that crazy woman Mukazano had slipped into my bed.

If someone were to ask me today why I ran away from the City of Blue Angels, I wouldn't know what to reply. In reality there was no

46

reason or, rather, yes, there was; there's always a good reason behind every stupid act. In all honesty, I hadn't gone there to stay. I had gone because Claudine had asked me to and, why hide it, because I entertained the vague hope that she'd be with me and that at night when the others were asleep and the dogs had stopped barking, she'd ask me to join her in her bed. What a joke! . . . Oh, sure, I was glad to have enough to eat, to sleep in a real bed without being attacked by mosquitoes and rats. It's just that I didn't imagine things would be the way they were. A life without commotion, without drugs, without rolls in the hay exists only in the seminary, and yet! From the start the thought of running away had been with me. But something kept me from making a decision; perhaps it was the weekly showing of a movie or maybe the famous screams that had intrigued me right away. In spite of my self-control, my first disagreements with the Hirish woman proved to be inevitable.

She came to see me one evening when I was on the swing staring at the stars and humming the old war songs my father had taught me.

'It's time, Faustin!' she said.

'That's for sure!' I replied naïvely, thinking that, since the world has been the world, it has always been time.

But she didn't appear to understand very well. And she seemed to get nervous.

'Let's go!' she yelled on the verge of throwing a fit.

'But where, ma'am?'

'If you must know everything, it's time to go to bed.'

'I'm not sleepy yet. It's barely dusk.'

'The others are already asleep.'

'How can you expect us to all get sleepy at the same time? We don't have the same eyelids; we don't have the same dreams.'

That's how the Hirish woman was. Over there, in her country, people got sleepy at the same time, felt hunger pangs at the same instant, and give or take a second, they felt the urge to urinate all at once. I quickly realized it was useless to explain to her that here it was different, that we each lived according to our own time, even to sharpen our machetes. The bitch knew my weak spot. With every incident, she'd call Claudine, and since I didn't want to hurt her, I'd toe the line, swearing to myself that the next time I'd lay waste to the henhouse then run away. And since finally I had, more or less, assembled my family, the opportunity was near. One morning, I slipped into the henhouse, wrung the necks of a dozen chickens, and hid them in the jute sacks Bizimungu used for his bread delivery. I woke the young ones. Under the truck's tarpaulin, we were as invisible as in the cave of this rascal Ali Baba our schoolmaster used to tell us about. Bizimungu pulled away without noticing our presence. He got out to announce his arrival to the baker on Mille Collines Avenue. We jumped down without being seen.

★   ★

Nothing had changed at HQ. Musinkôro was overjoyed, probably because of the amount of food I was bringing. We had a joint to celebrate our reunion, and the whole family gathered in the living room.

'I see you picked up some game on the way,' said Musinkôro alluding to my companions. 'This little one?'

'It's not what you think, friend. The girls are my sisters, and he's my little brother, Ambroise.'

'You're kidding! Who's got brothers left?'

'Well, I do. I must be luckier than the others.'

'Oh, so you think it's a stroke of luck to have three mouths to feed?'

He slipped his hands in the jute sacks and yelled out to everyone, 'Joséphina, Emilienne, Tatien, pluck these chickens. Use some for today's soup, and you can roast the rest for the next days. . . . You did well, Faustin; things aren't as before.'

He rolled another joint and bitterly told me about M. Van der Poot. M. Van der Poot was well known to everyone in the city long before this grim affair about customs and mores befell him. M. Van der Poot was not only white but Flemish and Belgian as well, which meant that he was three times more likely than others to disregard our own way of life. Yet he had been living in Rwanda long before the *advents*. He knew by heart the names of our hills, our intertribal passions, and the songs of our drunkards. No one could appreciate *umutsima* (our banana paste), zebra steak, and spirits of sorghum like him. He was a good family man who sang at church with his children and who loved his wife so much that he would nibble her lips in the middle of the street. But it wasn't just his wife he loved; he also loved swindlers and paralytics, the elderly and children, even, according to gossip, the whores on rue du Mont-Kabuyé. He especially liked the children! It was often reported that he was not just a technician but also an incorrigible *pedrophile*.

He worked for the Belgian agency. His wife was also a technician. As I see it, whites lead a double life; at home, they take charge of their careers; here, they take charge of ours. Go figure why after such a long time M. Van der Poot still didn't understand anything about our customs and mores. Here, Monsieur Van der Poot, when a man wants a girl, he gives her parents some sorghum and some beer, and he deflowers her with the whole tribe's knowledge, and when there is no tribe, he jumps her in the nearest ditch without preliminaries and without getting caught. But you, you got caught! By whom? By Froduald, the policeman, who, to tell the truth, was only trying to make ends meet. But that night you had too much Johnny Walker, and as a result you got agitated for no reason. This time you refused to grease the hand of that sly Froduald.

'The price of a beer, Monsieur Van der Poot, only the price of a beer!'

'Nothing doing, monkey! I've decided I'm not going to pay any more. At this rate, a person could go broke. Why don't you go hunt topis, that is if you know how to use your rifle. After all a rifle is mechanical. It's not as easy to handle as a machete for cutting cane.'

That sounded a lot like a breach of contract. Froduald didn't work his balls off in the hallways of the Mille Collines Hotel just to ensure their security. He was also in charge of alerting the young girls begging under the flame trees of the tourist office and the national park when an opportunity presented itself. Once she was in the room, he was the one who paced up and down the halls in his ragged fatigues and his sawed-off shotgun to intimidate voyeurs and the housekeepers. That was well worth a small coin and a little consideration. But you had too much Johnny Walker and fifteen years among us hadn't totally accustomed you to our tropical whims. The tornadoes, the flies, the odors of smoke-dried meats and rancid butter, the sidewalks infected with urine would make you fly off the handle. You'd accidentally blurt out cusswords and profanities: 'Ouakaris, bononos, caterpillar, and lizard eaters!' That day you called Froduald 'nippled rogue'! Nippled rogue! Oh, Monsieur Van der Poot! To crown it all, you had been sent that scabby little Emilienne, who had no equal when it came to hastening someone's downfall. She began to roll on the floor screaming (in the meantime having quickly painted her vagina with chicken blood she kept in a tube and carried with her at all times) as soon as Froduald had blown his whistle and shot a bullet into the elevator door to signal the alarm. The police chief, Théodomir, had been keeping an eye on you since you had called his sister-in-law Immaculée (the florist on avenue de la République) a sack of shit and a portly black lump. And you were still drunk. You said some mean things about our police force, 'a cabal of scoundrels,' and about our army, 'the ghostly legion!' It's best not to mention the name of the vermin that according to you crawl through the pubic hair of our women and the name of the diseases you say eats away their butts. It was so offensive that Chief Théodomir chose to simply smile.

'Go ahead, crawfish, go ahead, talk crap all you want! Rest assured that I'm not going to have you deported; that would be too easy!'

And there you are. One hundred lashes and seven nights in a prison cell with junkies and petty criminals. So you began to cry like a child without even bothering to hide your eyes. Only, a white man crying doesn't even elicit pity. It's true, however, that around here we'd never seen whites crying, as if all the tears in the world were reserved for us blacks. The prisoners, the policemen, everyone pointed at you and laughed. And outside the bars of your cell, this birdbrain Emilienne who had scratched her face and her thighs was showing her thing to everyone and yelling louder than the muezzin. She told about the number of times she had tried to resist before yielding to your rutting animal assaults: 'What do you expect, ten years old and dealing with a fat pig like him?' Those who had rushed over were noisily approving. Some proposed cutting you up starting with the guilty organ, others dipping you naked in a vat of boiling oil. 'What better fate for a crawfish?' the usually stern Chief Théodomir had exclaimed.

The matter had made headlines in newspapers as far as Uganda. But your country was able to get permission to have you transferred to a room at the La Mise Hotel while awaiting more detailed information, with orders that you report every morning to Chief Théodomir. You were lucky, Monsieur Van der Poot. You would have been thrown in jail, and I would have done worse to you than what got me in the Juniors' Club right now. No kidding, Monsieur Van der Poot! No kidding!

⋆ ⋆

Now, our guys, they're definitely not *pedrophiles*. In fact they can't have an opinion on the subject since they don't know what that means. There's nothing more natural in our hills than to marry a pubescent girl or, if we live in the city, to jump her at the first opportunity. We see one going down the street? We don't just ogle her, we feel her butt, we fondle her breasts without fear of judges or the staunch eye of Christ. And if in the meantime the boldest ones unbutton their flies or venture some inane remarks, those present will just laugh (to each his own customs and mores, Monsieur Van der Poot). The first time I learned about that was when I was with my sisters in front of the Caritas Bookstore. Lewd faces appeared behind picture windows, motorcycles tooted, cars abruptly put on the brakes when they got near us. Obviously I must have been transformed into a troll or a clown! In this type of situation, you don't understand right away. My first reaction was to examine my rags in case something unusual had nested there. Well, no; the leers and the racket were not for me. Without my noticing it, Esther and Donatienne had become women. A gnawing anger mixed with an incomprehensible feeling of shame took hold of me. These fevered looks directed at their bodies reminded me of a swarming of caterpillars on a newborn's back. That was the day I decided to have a gun too.

'What are you aiming at, silly boy?' Sembé asked me when I confided in him. 'If you're thinking of the post office or the Bank of Rwanda, don't count on me.'

'Take me to your supplier or sell me your gun.'

'That'll cost you twenty thousand but I insist on being kept informed.'

'It only concerns me.'

'Oh, I see! You plan to keep the Hirish woman's pile of money for yourself? I thought we were friends!'

'The Hirish woman's pile of money?'

'Don't pretend you don't know! Every Monday her driver, Bizibungu, takes her to the Banque Africaine Continentale to pick up her operating budget for the week. Taking care of two hundred motherless and fatherless young ones, that must require quite a kitty, right?'

'I don't like the Hirish woman much, but I would never do that to her. If I weren't so ungrateful, I should be calling her Mama.'

'Oh, all those poor women who've been our mamas!'

Claudine's second visit wasn't as reassuring.

'I'm sorry it took so long for me to come back to visit you, but, you understand, I had to see the judge.'

'So?'

'So, things are not that simple.'

'Are they going to hang me or throw me to the hyenas?'

'You're never so detestable as when you're trying to be funny. For the moment, there's no talk of hanging you but rather of moving your case along. It'll take one year, two years, who knows?'

'In short I've been given a respite.'

'You call that a respite, with all this sickness going around!' (She looked away and furtively touched her eye – did she want to wipe a tear? – before going on.) 'Rest assured, I'll do everything I can to get you out of here!'

'What can I get?'

'The judge told me there are three categories of guilty individuals: the accomplices (zero to five years), those who carry out the deed (five to twenty years) and the organizers (life or the gallows). However, you're a special case. You've always been a special case, Faustin Nsenghimana!'

She had said that with a hint of ferocity, as if she wanted to be delivered of something. Perhaps she had finally decided to see me as I really was: a real bastard and not the little martyr her complicated mind had invented for itself. She sighed, obviously unable to hide something, but what? Her weariness in front of the jailers and the judges, her exasperation or, more coldly put, the disgust that the shady character I was inspired in her? Her lips parted but no sound came out of her mouth. She looked toward the broken windowpane and the rotting wood of the door. She must be telling herself: 'Call the jabirus, stop these stupid visits once and for all, move on to what is really my business, what really matters.' I shivered. To look the other way was counterproductive: I was afraid of losing her. It's like that, even when you're irredeemable, even when you're in hell, you need someone as a link to the world. Especially since in my case, this someone was named Claudine, a chick with a big wallet, marvelous eyes, and a pair of buttocks so gifted they drew the eyes of a whole street. She willingly let the silence continue, as if to make me understand how far my detestable temperament could lead us. What to do in such cases but play with your ragged shirttail while twisting your mouth?

'Er . . .' I finally said. 'HQ . . . Do you go by HQ sometimes?'

Only the awkwardness of the moment could make me say that. HQ. I wanted only one thing: to erase it from my memory since that blasted night when I fled with dogs at my heels. All those who lived there had become ghosts for me, even Esther, even Donatienne, even my little brother, Ambroise. That's how it is.

'HQ? But . . . there is no more HQ. That evening the police kicked them all out . . . I told you that Sembé is dead, right?'

'Yes!'

'Don't ask me news of your brother and sisters. I have none myself.'

It must have been a trick so she could distance herself from me even more. I tried to snare her with the first hook I could think of. 'Thank you for the lawyer . . . and for the rest.'

'It's nothing. It's strange that you've never asked me news of Una. Although it's true that you never ask about anyone . . .'

'So, what's become of her?'

'I don't really know; India, Cambodia, or perhaps Somalia. She left Rwanda almost a year ago.'

'And the City of Blue Angels, does it still exist?'

'More or less. Its walls are slowly crumbling since it's been palmed off on the state . . . Oh, none of this would have happened if you'd stayed at the City of Blue Angels! If you get out of here, you'll go back won't you?'

'What a question!'

She stroked my hair with less maternal sympathy than usual. That made me feel good. She continued talking while her hand rested on my neck.

'I'll get you out of here. It's not your fault. No, you're not such a bad sort; it's the times.'

More than ever I wanted her. I managed to curb my impulses. Otherwise my lips would have jumped on her mouth, my hands would have gotten lost in her large breasts. But she couldn't guess my intentions. She was smiling at me. Was it on purpose that her shining eyes had remained fixed on me, expressing for poor little me, maybe not the all-consuming passion I hoped for, but at least some compassion, the sincere feelings of a woman? In spite of my rags encrusted with filth, my skin speckled with the mange, my odor of dead dog.

'Here, I brought you this,' she said before leaving.

She handed me a package wrapped in brown paper. It was soap, toothpaste, toothbrushes, a comb, plus a pair of shoes and a splendid cotton safari jacket.

'You see that I think about you. So I'll return as soon as possible. Trust me, I'll rush the lawyer and the judge; I'll move heaven and earth.'

She seemed so sincere that, once back in my cell, when I was asked the name of the good fairy who had dressed me this way, I replied jauntily, 'My fiancée, of course! You'll see how everything will be easy the day you have one too.'

⋆   ⋆

From that day forward and until my catastrophic performance in court, she came to see me almost every Friday and never empty-handed. The warden had given me permission to go outside with her, way in the back of the yard, under the eucalyptus tree against the north section of the wall, to taste the dishes she would bring me. Sometimes we'd stay there the whole afternoon. When I asked for sorghum cereals, I was sure to have some at her next visit; same for beans in cow butter or ubugari, our delicious manioc paste, so filling, in fact, that a person can survive a whole week without swallowing anything more. Besides grub, there was always a little surprise for me: a carton of Ambassadeur cigarettes, a liter of banana beer or a box of honey candy. She had actually decided to comb my hair and cut my nails herself. Imagine – she had bribed the chief cook so he'd bring me a pail of water. That way, I could take a shower – a real one – in the metal cubbyhole that served as a bathroom for the jabirus. None of this is allowed, of course. But, as my good father, Théoneste, used to say: 'Life's flavor is in the forbidden fruit, even whites know that!' Life is an odd obstacle race: all the hedges are forbidden, so why are people born if not to jump them? And believe me, there's nothing that so resembles life as a prison. Take for example here; spitting on the floor, disrespecting the jabirus, committing a sin of the flesh, stealing from someone, and bumping off one's neighbor are not permitted. At first it was even prohibited to wear one's own clothes, bring food in the cells, or smoke. But since these famous *advents*, everything works upside down. Everyone strives to break the rules.

When I say rules, of course, I mean the administration's. The laws of the milieu are inviolable; the least deviation is settled between men, meaning with a knife. No one is safe from the knife, not even someone with protection like little old me; that's the lesson to remember when first entering here. Dysentery and malaria are less rife and kill more slowly than being stabbed with a knife. You have to always be on guard. Sleep is the most frightening time! Since I've been here, I wake up suddenly ten times a night, sweating, calling my mother for help (my new status as a condemned man did not change that). At first, I thought that was caused, to use the Hirish woman's word, by the *taumatrisms* I had undergone. But the Hirish woman couldn't understand. It's hard to talk with whites; our worlds were made as if the feet of one were the head of the other. They're francophones, belgeophones, or swissophones. But all we speak is Kinyarwanda. Hutus, Tutsis, Twas, everyone speaks Kinyarwanda. I had tried to explain that to her the night we were on the swing. And do you know what she replied, this *umuzungu* slut as we call those of her race around here? 'That didn't work so well for you! Why don't you speak several languages and maybe you'll understand each other better!' Well, she can roast in India, Madame the Hirish woman! Because it's not a matter of languages or a matter of *taumatrisms*, it's a matter of knives. It's not because that warthog of a corporal took away my kite at the church nor because of what happened to my brothers that I have delirium at night. It's fear of the knife. I've reached the point where I don't care if I die. But, God almighty, not by the blade of a knife!

*   *

Why the devil didn't I arm myself? With the money and the cigarettes Claudine was giving me, I could have amassed an arsenal, just to discourage the big thugs. Sometimes I miss my pretty little revolver. If I were asked what happened to it, I wouldn't know what to reply. I think I might have thrown it away in one of the cornfields bordering the shantytowns of Muhima so I could run better that accursed night when my destiny changed radically. 'The child knows how to run but he doesn't know how to hide.' If I had remembered those ancient words, I would have gone directly to the police instead of wasting their time.

I could kill Tatien! At least that's what I was thinking when I set foot in the Juniors' Club. Now I'm not so sure, even if by some miracle I were to get out of here. In prison you don't lose just your hair and your fingernails, you also lose your basic instincts. Without realizing it you begin to burn what you loved yesterday and worship what used to seem despicable. In any case, is it really Tatien's fault? With him or without him, they would have found me anyway. And I had plenty of time to flee. It took them three weeks to find my hiding place. I could have easily reached Burundi or Tanzania since Rwanda is a tiny country (two elephant strides at most, not even a giant step). I could have met my parents at Gabiro or Kigembe. We would have come across old Funga wandering through the euphorbia and ficus forests conversing with the spirits. . . . Only, I didn't have the heart to go back on the road. The orchids must not have the same scents nor the prickly pear trees the same leaves on their limbs. Besides in one village I would have been called *génocidaire* and in another, informer. It's just as well that things happened the way they did. If one must die, better to do it like the old elephants, in a familiar place and without putting out too much effort. I also have a great advantage: Claudine is not far away. All the heroes I saw on TV at the Fraternité Bar died in the arms of their beloved. Without actually being one myself, I wouldn't mind ending my days in Claudine's arms. But will they think to inform her once they've set up the gallows? Maybe one or two weeks later. I can see her leaning over the common grave, whispering to the warden: 'Oh, young Faustin Nsenghimana! His end was at least better than his friend Sembé's.'

★   ★

She often returned to the subject of my quarrel with the Hirish woman. I suspected her of still holding a grudge against me for leaving the City of Blue Angels, and in so doing, offending her dear friend.

'You know she often talked to me about you before she left. If you hadn't been so mule-headed!'

In truth, I had a grudge against myself also – oh, not for leaving the City of Blue Angels, but for doing so without letting her know. I was ashamed. So to avoid her after running away, I preferred leaving my little family with Tatien in front of the Caritas Bookstore so I could do my gleaning in the Méridien Hotel area. That's where I met Rodney. He didn't tell me right away that he was English. He spoke Swahili, which I understand.

'If I asked you to take me to a whorehouse, I'm sure you'd be willing!'

'How can you tell, Bwana?'

'The way you wriggle your nose. It's immediately obvious that you like to sniff out money. So, little brother, are you with me or would you rather I give all this to someone else?'

In his hand was a twenty-dollar bill, which he held tight between his thumb and his index finger so I could see that it was no joke.

'There's no use humiliating your junior. With or without money, I would have taken you anyway. Imana is our god, and I swear to it before Imana.'

'I don't doubt it. I bet you'll take it anyway. The world is full of nice people. But I don't know anyone who would refuse a dollar, even for the noblest of motives. So get in!'

He was already sitting at the wheel of his Mitsubishi Pajero and was busy opening the passenger door for me. You can well imagine he didn't have to ask me twice to get in. If he was telling the truth, I would have the means to take care of HQ for several weeks. I'd finally be able to give Ambroise the ball he'd been wanting. Children have this advantage: they have no sense of tragedy. Life is still a game even in times of disasters.

'Where to, little brother?'

Where was my mind? I hadn't even thought about it. The truth is, there are no more whorehouses in Kigali. The *advents* did away with everything that really matters: markets, churches, offices, recreation centers, and whorehouses, too. It would take time for all that to be rebuilt. However, you had to be stupid to think that this dissolute town would take up abstinence, anyway just long enough to acquire a new red light district. I remembered that one day by chance I had followed a group of drunks to a strange place in the northern districts. Life had taught me that a lot could be learned from a drunk. You just have to follow one to ensure your survival. By the fourth glass, there's no one more generous on earth. When the bar is lively, the owner knows his stuff and there are plenty of decent chicks, and if you're just a little bit cunning – that is, if you know how to be discreet – you can be well taken care of. You eat and you drink for free, and those little coins so hard to find when you're washing cars drop willingly into your pockets. If a woman shows the least bit of interest in him, there he goes yelling: 'Hey kid, why don't you go buy me some roast chicken and some cigarettes! Get some for the lady too and be sure to keep the change!'

So this strange place was a very respectable bistro. There were no drugs sold there or any of this adulterated whisky imported from Uganda. The owner, whose name was Clementine, must have been a secretary in a previous life. The patrons were sales representatives and office managers. The women who frequented the place had never plied their trade before. They were all respectable mothers who came looking for company and, well, a little money to take care of their brood since the husband wasn't around anymore; he was either in jail because he was found guilty of genocide or in a common grave if it was the other way around. With a little bit of savoir-faire, you could get one of them to follow you if you looked clean and gave the impression that your pockets measured up to the situation. I couldn't quite remember where the place was. Nevertheless, I instinctively answered and with much confidence, 'Go toward Kacyiru, my friend.'

'What is that, another district, another town, or another country?'

'Another district. Is this your first time in Rwanda?'

'My very first time, kid, or I wouldn't have offered you twenty dollars to show me the way to a whorehouse.'

'Where do you come from?'

'That's the first thing people ask you when they meet you. I come from the hotel near here and I've already told you where I'd like to go.'

'Don't tell me you're Hirish!'

'No, that would be the other side: English. But I was born in Uganda, I grew up in Bombay, and I don't live in London. I live in Nairobi.'

'What kind of work do you do in Nairobi?'

'Don't ever repeat that word! I hate work. I spend my time sleeping or hunting crocodiles; I sell their skins after I've enjoyed their meat. And since that's not enough to keep me supplied with all the drinks

I want and to support my numerous mistresses, I hire myself out as a cameraman when I can. Did you understand or do you want me to repeat it?'

'All right, big brother! No need to get mad. Here when you meet a stranger, you don't try to understand, you ask him where he comes from. That's what we call being polite.'

'In Bombay, in Djakarta, in Dublin, and in Honolulu also. And it's not always polite.'

'Cameraman, that's like the movies?'

'I make films, but for television. There's an earthquake in Columbia and Rodney's there. A strong monsoon in India, and here comes weird Rodney and his strange gear. A massacre in Somalia, they call Rodney. Rodney is everywhere there's trouble. Rodney is a doctor who arrives hoping things are even worse. And as you can see, Rodney's fit as a fiddle. Ha! Ha!'

'So your name's Rodney? You have a pretty name and a funny laugh. I'm Faustin.'

'You're also fit as a fiddle, Faustin. I won't ask you how you do it but you're on the right track. It's better when it's others who croak, don't ever forget that, Faustin. After thirty years in Africa, I don't know any proverbs. But if I had to invent one, it would be this one: 'Pierre's tears? Honey for Rodney.''

'Why are you just now coming to Rwanda?'

'Why, why? I don't know. I'm just a bloody old wretch, Faustin; I come only when I'm called. And this time no one called me. And yet I won't say I was starving but I could have used a bundle of dough.'

'There's nothing much left to see.'

'Don't you believe it, little brother; there's always something to see. If need be, you make it up. That's the gift of a cameraman: always give something to see, even if there's nothing to show.'

'Kenyan television sent you?'

'With what means? If you're going to howl with the wolves, might as well do it with the strongest. I came with the BBC. And what did I learn this morning? CNN and Swiss television are soliciting my services. The prospect of three weeks of work. We must celebrate that!'

'You'll stay the whole time in Kigali?'

'I suppose that we'll do what they call the genocide sites. Industrial sites, tourist sites, now genocide sites! . . . What can I say, mon frère, the dead are big stars, even if all they have left is their skull. Do you know some genocide sites?'

'Er . . . I know them all.'

'Have you ever worked for a radio or television station?'

'Er . . . yes!'

'Which one?'

'Er . . . Hirish television.'

'Irish television, hey . . . Well, I'm going to ask those in charge if they need a guide to visit the genocide sites.'

And that's how I met Rodney. With the help of several passersby, I finally found the famous bar. The last time I was there, it had no name. Now across its front was a sign with a blue background and yellow letters. Written on it was: 'Catch As Catch Can.' Thank goodness, the owner hadn't changed, making my task easier.

'Madame Clementine, I'm bringing you a customer,' I yelled as soon as I was inside.

I wanted to prevent any misunderstandings since people like me aren't readily admitted to reputable places. At first she frowned, then her face brightened when she noticed behind me what I was bringing her. For barmaids and whores, whites are as important as the Messiah. They have the power of money. And besides, they don't brawl. Also, they're more tender in bed. It's even said that they never have AIDS. They never ask for credit, they say hello and good-bye, and they leave big tips. They're not like the idiots from around here.

'Come on in,' Clementine replied. 'Take the table in the back; I assure you, you'll be better there. At the bar, there's too much noise; all this drunken music and the voices of big liars.'

But already Rodney was seated on the only free stool among the drunks.

'My dear lady, where there's noise, there's life.'

'A philosopher; we've got a philosopher here,' the dear lady laughed. 'What do you need?'

While the waiter was serving the orders, I took that time to whisper a few words in Clementine's ear. A gleam of greed filled her eyes.

'Oh, really? . . . What kind of woman does he want? You sort of know the place, which one would he really like: Solange or Benedictine?'

I answered 'Solange,' as if I remembered her. She was a beautiful Tutsi who had grown up in Nairobi. Her husband, a soldier with the RPF, had died at the battle of Byumba. She had the smile of an angel and she spoke English. Rodney was delighted with her. He slipped me the twenty dollars and gave me a pack of cigarillos.

'Now, hurry up and drink a beer, then get lost,' he shouted.

'He's not strong enough yet,' suggested Solange. 'Better just a Coke.'

'Bah! Let him get sloshed if that's his pleasure. In Manilla I saw boys younger than him empty half pints of whisky before smoking crack. So drink this and scoot, little man. You can see I don't need your company anymore. Now that you're rich, go wherever you want to sniff your glue or stick a needle in your arm. Do it to your heart's content, just don't do it where I can see you. It's not morality making me say this. It's so I won't have anything to reproach myself for in case you croak. I hope you don't sell your little behind? . . . Well that's something at least. Try to be at the hotel tomorrow at seven; I'll see what I can do for you.'

★ ★

'Musinkôro,' I said to my old friend, 'watch over Esther, Donatienne, and Ambroise. I might be away from Kigali for a week or two, I don't know yet. Don't ask me why, I wouldn't be able to tell you. And, to be honest, I don't feel like it.'

'Oh,' he exclaimed. 'You've found a cushy deal and you don't want to share, is that it?'

I handed him part of the money I had time to exchange at the market with the traffickers we pompously called *busenessmen* and jumped out a window so he wouldn't hold me back.

I was at the Méridien Hotel around six o'clock. I waited at the entrance with the drowsy doormen, the cigarette venders, and the shoeshines. I spied Rodney's Pajero and kept my eye on it. I knew there was no way in the world I'd be admitted to the lobby. That's how it is. The sun helping, I also dozed off. The opportunity would have slipped through my fingers if I hadn't been awakened by an incredible racket. It was coming from the hotel lobby where the whole town population seemed to have convened to hurl abuse at each other and throw punches. I squeezed my way through the crowd and climbed up on the reception desk so I could see better. The scene was pathetic: Rodney, in his jockey shorts, and Solange, half-naked, were fighting like cats and dogs while vigorously swearing at each other.

'This whore stole my money!'

'That's not true; he's the one who won't pay me!'

And the crowd, which appeared to want to separate them, was actually throwing oil on the fire so the two could beat each other up even more.

'You women, as soon as you see a white man you spread your thighs. You got just what you deserved. If you'd given yourself to me, none of this would have happened to you.'

'Why don't you blame the white man. Why would a man like him get mixed up with the first woman he sees? And at the Méridien, no less. Geez!'

'Search her purse,' bellowed Rodney. 'My money's in there! I'll prove it: I paid her twenty dollars with two tens. I lost five hundred dollars; four in hundreds and a fifty plus ten fives.'

I dove on the purse lying at the feet of the protagonists and opened it in front of everyone.

'Look,' I told the receptionist, 'count this money to see if he's telling the truth.'

At that instant, Rodney, noticing my presence, shouted in obvious relief.

'Oh, there you are? If only you'd been here earlier . . . I was watching for you through the blinds in my room when she stole my money.'

The racket lasted another fifteen minutes, each spectator insisting on providing an opinion on the gravity of the matter and what further actions should be taken. Finally everyone agreed that Rodney was right. His money was returned to him.

'Blast,' he said once we were outside. 'The bastards have left! Have you ever heard of a small village called Nyarubuyé?'

⋆ ⋆

I knew Nyarubuyé was toward the north in some remote region of swamps and lakes serving as a border between Rwanda and Tanzania. I must have seen it on a map at school. And my dear old father, Théoneste, must have proclaimed that fact during one of those nights when, after a good harvest, he would compose songs for his cows and recreate scenes from our ancient epics. That's the area I'd have gone through if I had gone to see Uncle Sentama – if I hadn't let myself be taken in by Thaddeus's scheme. I had never been there. In fact, outside of one or two trips to Kigali, I had never left my native province of Bugesera before the *advents*. But there was no reason to tell pal Rodney. From the day Corporal Nyumurowo snatched my kite from my hands, I learned that playing the innocent serves no purpose. My rascally father Théoneste's fable is still fresh in my mind: 'Lying and Truth are the first inhabitants of the earth. Truth is the older brother but since Lying is more gifted, well, he's the one who runs the world. Don't you ever forget that, kid.'

We reached Nyarubuyé after an hour of blacktop roads and an endless number of bush trails that were never the right ones. The BBC guys made no comments when they saw us arrive. They must have forgotten all about our tremendous lateness and the shameful incident of the morning. They had parked their Land Rovers on a slope and had taken over the only café around; they were gobbling up corned-beef sandwiches and drinking huge quantities of warm beer. There must have been ten of them, including one woman who had no clue she was a woman because her behavior and her clothes were a lot like that of her companions.

'Don't worry, Rodney, we saved you a case,' she said. 'And if that's not enough to quench your thirst, the barman assured us he has a couple dozen in stock in a warehouse at the other end of the village. Did you see the monkeys in the cypress forest, and not far from there, the grottos?'

'Well, no, Jenny. My guide took another route.'

She lifted her cap so she could observe me better. I must have looked strange in my old pants held up with pins and my sneakers full of holes because a little laugh softened her face, which I found particularly masculine.

'So that's the man you told us about,' she exclaimed. 'What's your name, young man?'

'Faustin. Faustin Nsenghimana, madame.'

'Don't call me madame, I hate that! Do like Rodney, call me Jenny. Tell me, were you born here, Faustin?'

'Er . . . Yes, madame.'

'Jenny, but that's okay. Are your parents from here?'

'Yes.'

'Where are they?'

'They're with the others.'

'At the co-op?'

'No, with the other skulls.'

She shivered and lowered her head. The blood rushed to her face giving her the complexion of a red pepper. I was glad to unnerve her like that. She wasn't the strongest after all.

'In the shed or at the church?' asked the one wearing radio earphones.

'In the banana groves, perhaps?' added the one who looked like JR and was writing notes in his spiral notebook.

'They say there are also some in the schoolyard and under the big kapok tree.'

'That's it, under the big kapok tree.'

I was becoming interesting. They abandoned their big Primus bottles and their sandwiches to pounce on their movie and photo cameras. They sat me down on an old metal chair and gathered around me. I had become as famous as Roger Milla.

'Why do you say 'under the big kapok tree'?' Jenny insisted with obvious interest that nevertheless had a hint of suspicion.

'They dragged them in that direction.'

'Who?'

'The Interharamwe.'

That's when things went downhill. My status went from star to accused. The cameras came closer to my face and the questions became more detailed, trickier. One had barely finished asking me something when another was already formulating a new question.

'Where were you on this famous day, the twelfth? . . . Were you alone? . . . What did you notice? . . . What time did the first militias arrive? . . . Why didn't the army do anything?'

Rodney finally became annoyed and interceded at the right moment.

'I found this child all alone, so go easy or I'm leaving the group. Tell me, Faustin, why didn't they kill you?'

'I fled.'

'Which way?'

'That way, toward the hills.'

'From those hills, would you have seen your parents being kidnapped under the big kapok tree?' asked Jenny indignantly. 'That doesn't add up. The big kapok tree is south, totally in the opposite direction. No one can see it from the hills, even from the very top. Besides the roofs and the banana plants, there are these tall attics in the center of the village that obstruct the view. We spotted the location before you came.'

'Ask him to show us his parents' house,' barked the big chubby one as he removed his earphones. 'By the way: Manchester four, Newcastle two!'

'That's it,' JR agreed. 'Let him show us his house.' 'In truth, I don't remember anymore.'

'Do you think Auschwitz survivors remember the life they led before landing in hell?' Rodney asked. 'Faustin, isn't this your first time back in your village?'

'The very first.'

'I see. I suggest we set up tents to get a little sleep and let this poor child collect his wits. I'm sure his account will be better than that of all these adults who won't fail to pester us with the why and the how of all that's happened. This kid has lived through things and with the eyes of a child. Out of the mouths of babes . . .'

Rodney unfolded a cot in his own tent but felt it necessary to hand me a bar of soap before extinguishing the lantern.

'Lying is as easy as breathing for you, Faustin! Not that it's necessarily a bad thing, unless you lie to me. For now, everything's fine. However, try not to lay it on too thick. The kapok tree incident almost sank us. Think long and hard before getting one out. I'll say it one more time, if you lie to Rodney, Rodney will whip your butt! Faustin, why do you have a gun?'

The next day, they gave me a copious lunch before filming me amid skulls stacked on tables, amid bones and bloody clothes stuffed in plastic bags or scattered in fields filled with debris. They showed me the convicted *génocidaires* sentenced, among other punishments, to repair the church roof that, in their unquenchable fury after all their victims were dead, they stubbornly destroyed. Jenny came near me and said, 'Now, think carefully, Faustin. Which one killed your parents?'

'I tell you that there were several. But I recognize this one, the one with a cone head and a piece of manioc in his mouth; he's the one who murdered my father.'

'Do you recognize any others?'

'Er . . . yes, the one with the club foot and the corn cigarette butt over his ear; that's the one who raped my mother . . .' (I started to bawl, just like Rodney had recommended). 'You can't mistake someone with a club foot.'

That lasted a week, and when we left the BBC people, I had become as good an actor as those I used to see on the TV at the Fraternité Bar, writhing and falling off horses as if they had been hit by real bullets.

Swiss television took us to Rebero, CNN, to Bisesero. It's as if pal Rodney's and my renown had become worldwide. The Norwegians dragged us to Musha, the Australians, to Mwuliré. I didn't need directions anymore. Rodney would set up his camera and the film rolled all by itself. In places where I had never set foot, I'd immediately recognize the charred hovel my parents had been dragged out of; the yard filled with hibiscus where their hamstrings had been slashed; the church hall where they had been murdered; the old wooden brewery where their blood had been used to make banana beer; the stove where their ears and intestines had been roasted and seasoned with peppers to serve as meals for the attacking forces, who had proved to be the bravest. I'd remove my cap to show the scars across my head, lift my old sweater to expose the machete cuts on my shoulders and my torso. Some film directors would shed tears. So then I'd invent some heroic deeds to move them even more. I'd describe how I had been able to repel my assailants, to jump on a bicycle lying around and pedal through the bush to the nearest forest. Then Rodney, with a satisfied smile, would promptly raise his thumb to show that it was good but it was over, and we'd do it again somewhere else.

Oh, if only that had lasted just three weeks as Rodney thought, I wouldn't be where I am now. No, it lasted a month and a half. I slept and ate for free, met important people, traveled without spending a cent. How many dollars did I collect: three hundred, four hundred? I'd be able to open a beauty salon, which, ever since I'd been in Kigali, I'd always secretly wanted. I was going to be rich!

I was far from knowing that God had decided on my perdition.

★ ★

'Misfortune is like rain: contrary to appearances, you never feel it,' old Funga used to tell me. 'It always comes in a succession of little things that accumulate, accumulate, and, one fine day, they overflow and there's water gushing from everywhere or else it's blood. Look, kid:

first it was young Gatoto who went insane, all alone in the hills while he was gathering wood; then it was Father Manolo, who collapsed in his car not long before dying at the pope's feet in front of the whole world since those people who film everything were all there; then it was the Italian woman who was slaughtered; and to top it all off, this airplane crash. People see only the incidents, never the thread that links them.' And old Funga was right. That day it actually was a succession of unimportant little things that led to my downfall. The worst part of it is that I came close to forgetting this accursed gun under a banana tree in Mwuliré. The night before, as usual, Rodney had put away his gear and set up his tent.

'Tonight, I'm going to sleep under the stars,' I told him.

That really intrigued him.

'Under the stars? . . . Oh shit, do as you please. It's not my body you'll be exposing to the mosquitoes.'

A big crescent moon was almost level with the hilltops visible in the east. The melodious sound of a flute could be heard in the distance. Calves lowed softly as they brushed against the shrubs nearby. That reminded me of the nights when I was a boy. All that was missing was the husky voice of my father (soaked with alcohol as was often the case) grappling with the wizard-kings and the valiant warriors of yesteryear and, of course, the tireless breathing of Mama struggling with her pots and pans between the hut and the well. I took my gun out of my pants, placed it by the banana tree, and stretched out on the grass. I intended to spend the night there without closing my eyes, without missing any of the scent of the flowers and the tiny sounds of nature. But the cool air of the hills soon got the better of me. The sun was high in the sky when I woke up. Rodney, who's always the last to get up, was snoring like a lamb. I shook his tent, and we left amid great confusion. That's why I forgot my gun.

We were back on the blacktop when I noticed I didn't have my gun. In truth, Rodney had not given me the time to look around, not even the time to think. Instead he gave me an earful because I didn't wake him up earlier. He had a lot of phone calls to make to Europe and Australia. He had to confirm his next day's flight for Nairobi. And then came the moment when I had to search my pockets to light a fag.

'Idiot!'

'Me?'

'No, Rodney, me. I forgot my gun!'

'Where?'

'Near the banana trees of Mwuliré'

The maniac came to a halt and without consulting me made a U-turn.

'It's not that important. I bought it just for appearances, but I've never used it for anything. With all the dollars you've given me, I could buy a dozen if I wanted to.'

'It's always serious when you lose something, dear little Faustin.'

On the way back, we had a flat near Rutongo. It must have been three or four o'clock in the afternoon. Rodney was getting agitated. He broke the jack. We had to wait thirty minutes before a kind soul stopped to help us. We reached the hotel around 5:00 P.M. He asked me to wait for him in front and, by the time he had washed up, packed his bags, turned in his rented Pajero and made his phone calls, it was 8:00 P.M. before he reappeared.

'And now, sonny, we're going to party!'

'Where?'

'At Catch As Catch Can, of course. I feel like making up with Solange. I like having nothing but good memories of a place where I've been.'

Clementine couldn't believe her eyes when she saw us coming.

'Oh, Monsieur Rodney, you really have gall! You humiliate my friend in front of all of Kigali and you dare come back here? Do you want to make her cry again or are you looking for more trouble?'

'No, madame, I've come to apologize. I admit I was a lout. I shouldn't have acted as I did. The truth is I was still drunk. All this noise for a little trifle. I should have let her keep the five hundred dollars. Do you think she'd accept them if I gave them back to her?'

'I'm afraid it's too late.'

'Oh, come on! Not only am I buying a round for the house but I'll slip you a hundred if you can manage to convince her. The season was rather good for the kid and me.'

'Money isn't everything. Solange isn't what you think. Before, Solange didn't know a bed other than her husband's. She didn't need to go out. She drank beer at home and ate her own cooking. That's the way it is for all of us in this world; no one knows what tomorrow will make of us.'

'We're in a bar, Clementine, not a church. Go wake Solange and tell her that I'm throwing myself at her feet.'

Clementine made a few attempts.

'There's no use my trying any more. She refuses to see you.'

'I want Solange and no one else!'

He banged on the counter and shouted a lot of rubbish. Everyone was drunk and there was a free-for-all. A police raid would first and foremost catch me. In the eyes of the law I was a vagrant and a minor. Besides I was the possessor of a wad of dollars wrapped in my shirttail and a firearm. They'd confiscate them, accuse me of theft, and throw me in jail. I got scared and slipped out.

I took the paths leading to Boulevard Nyabugogo. Behind me the echo of insults, punches, and bottles breaking let me know that the fight was taking a dramatic turn. Rodney must have broken someone's teeth or maybe he had been knocked senseless with a chair, unless it was with the iron bar that was used to barricade the door. I didn't care. I hadn't felt this good in a long time. Upon my word, when you have money in your pockets, nothing else counts. No, money doesn't bring you happiness. It is happiness! Once on the boulevard, I could whistle to myself and return to my usual pace, not giving a hoot for the dogs barking along the way or the couples moaning as they made love behind the thin mud and bamboo walls.

I walked into HQ on tiptoe. I didn't want to disturb anyone. I lit a candle and went toward the corner where my brother and my sisters used to sleep to make sure they were there. All I saw were two bodies stretched out on the mat. I woke Tatien up.

'Tatien, tell me where Esther is.'

'Faustin, you're back? At this hour! How unfortunate. You couldn't have chosen a worse time!'

I grabbed him by the collar and came close to strangling him.

'Tell me where Esther is!'

'Let go of me, you little thug! I'm not the one you need to be coming after. . . . In the next room. But, I beg you, don't go there!'

It's strange, I had never thought about it before, but as soon as he said that, I knew instinctively what I would discover a few seconds later: Esther naked on a straw mattress and Musinkôro sprawled on top.

I aimed at the hoodlum's head and fired until I ran out of bullets.

The third time Claudine came to visit me, she wasn't alone. A man, possibly in his sixties, a pipe stuck in his mouth, was seated next to her in the warden's office.

'This is the lawyer I told you about. He hasn't had time to come see you but he's been studying your file. Sit down. We can talk more comfortably.'

I didn't like the tone she was using at all. It wasn't hers. It was someone else's – quavering and cautious; it sounded foreign to me.

'Don't hide the truth from me, little sister. Tell me everything: have they sentenced me, yes or no?'

'You're acting like a child,' the lawyer growled without taking the trouble to remove the pipe from his mouth. 'Didn't prison teach you anything? No questions, no raising of the voice in front of one's elders. Don't you know? Even at the brink of the grave, you must keep your composure if you're a real man!'

Why did she choose that one? He had a little salt-and-pepper goatee that I hated, teeth blackened by tobacco that I hated, and a habit of speaking while snapping his fingers that I hated. Also, he behaved as if we were not in a prison but in his own living room and he was rounding off his umpteenth offspring's education. That didn't seem to bother Claudine. I had become the ungrateful son and she was the dutiful wife. She was quietly filing her nails as she observed us. She seemed to enjoy leaving me practically alone with this heartless man. My anger grew. My tongue began to move by itself in my mouth.

'It's obvious you're not the one about to be wiped out! I've learned enough in here that I can go before the judgment of God alone. A human eye will never scare me again. And believe me, big guy, I didn't have to try hard: it came by itself. Now, I'm leaving! I'm free to see whom I please, even in jail.'

It was as if I had just blasphemed. For the first time I noticed hatred in Claudine's eyes.

'You're going too far, Faustin! No one speaks like that to Monsieur Bukuru. It's out of friendship for me that he has agreed to defend you. Monsieur Bukuru has clients everywhere. He's in demand in Butaré, in Ruhengeri, everywhere, even outside the country. You're lucky to have Monsieur Bukuru all to yourself. He came expressly for you and you insult him, Faustin, you insult him, you, a kid! Don't disappoint me, Faustin, don't be ungrateful! Your father, Théoneste, must have told you not to blind the one who taught you to see. I . . .'

She burst into tears. I had witnessed lots of things the three years after my twelfth birthday. But that was too much. I wanted to jump in her arms and cry with her. That must be what love is. To cry, openly, and sincerely this time. Only, not a single tear came to dampen my eyes. I had lost that habit as I had lost the habit of swimming, trapping tree squirrels and ground squirrels, or washing my hands before meals. That's how it is. The one she called Monsieur Bukuru got up to hand her a tissue. Most certainly that wasn't enough to quell his base instincts. Playing the role of the one who comforts, he ran his hand over her shoulders, as if I didn't understand.

'Pull yourself together, dear lady. It's nothing. What matters is getting this little shit out of here.'

Deep down inside, I wanted to apologize, to make sure everything turned out all right. But my nerves were burning with rage. If the devil himself had taken hold of me, I wouldn't have been surprised. If I'd had a knife, I probably would have stuck it in Bukuru's belly.

'I'm sorry, my elder,' I replied. 'As far as this shit is concerned, little is better than big. It's the opposite for gold.'

He sat back down, his hands shaking. I enjoyed seeing him in such a state. If he'd had a heart attack, I would have felt really relieved.

'You see, mademoiselle, he insults me, yes, insults me! But that's all right, what matters is to get him out of here. Tell him what we've already done for him, you tell him!'

She turned toward me, let out a sigh that made her opulent chest quiver, and smiled at me as if nothing had happened.

'Listen, young Faustin. This is not a place for you. It's understandable that you're a little depressed. But soon, all this will be over. Your trial is next week. Aren't you pleased?'

⋆   ⋆

I made that kite all by myself with the Italian woman's wrapping paper. Back from the only vacation she'd taken since being among us, she appeared at our hut.

'Here, Théoneste, I brought back medications for your wife and fabric for your children. For you, there's a bottle of whiskey. I know

I shouldn't have. But I wanted to make you happy. And what makes Théoneste happy? A bottle of whiskey! That doesn't mean you should get drunk all night, however. I need you to vaccinate the hogs tomorrow. So thank you for your kindness. I noticed that my vegetable patch is neatly weeded and my cowsheds are clean. Oh, if only Théoneste drank less, Théoneste would be the best man of the village.'

My mother brought the fabric to Gicari the tailor, who made a pair of pants for me and some shifts for my sisters. I saved the pretty wrapping paper. It was multicolored and shiny, flexible enough to withstand the wind. It was just right for a kite. Our schoolteacher had taught us how to make kites. With a long string and some of this sap that burns your eyes collected from the tree called *imiyenzi*, I ended up with a magnificent hawk that looked real when it was aloft. My hawk would fly so high that it could have grazed the president's plane if it had flown near there. When I took it outside, all the kids ran behind me asking me to let them touch it. The old women would stand in front of their houses to admire Théoneste's son's 'strange gizmo.' My father didn't mind flaunting his pride, because for once there was a good reason for it. Only old Funga wasn't pleased.

'It would take just one gust of wind for your gizmo to brush up against the heavens. What if you dislodged a star, would you be able to put it back in its place? No! Be careful, Théoneste's son, you'll never be cleverer than the gods.'

I don't remember how old I was exactly: maybe seven, maybe eight. In those days, I didn't think it was necessary to count the years. There would be times when, tired of the necessity to forget, an adult would recall what had happened before: the bloodbaths of 1959, those of 1964, those of 1972, and so on, as Uncle Sentama would say. I didn't attach much importance to that. I just thought they were talking about some legend that would have occurred before this famous Flood so often evoked by Father Manolo and in a world other than mine. Life seemed good to me, even worthwhile, and very often fantastic. I served at Mass, went hunting with Father Manolo, helped the Italian woman in the cowsheds and the Brazilian nuns make almond candies that my sisters would sell on market day to help the orphans. On Sundays I'd score goals for the Juniors' Group and, in the evening, when I grew tired of the alcoholic ravings of my father, I'd go to the Fraternité Bar to watch a movie on the TV and leer at Augustine's backside. We weren't very respected because of my father's inanities and his inveterate fondness for the bottle but we were well liked. My mother was the kind of wife many would have loved to have – discreet, hard working, submissive to her husband like a contended slave. Nothing ever bothered her: not the chores the neighbors made us do nor the jibes directed at her husband. Actually, the village wasn't fair to Théoneste. He was a drunk, all right – like most of his neighbors, in fact – but he was an honest man who could do anything. A keep net to trap eels, a roof to repair, a field to weed, a hoe to patch up? You'd go see Théoneste with a flask of banana beer and it was as if the work was already done. His fields were the best tended of the village, and his swine, I swear, were so fat their bellies dragged the ground. His soul knew neither anger nor resentment. When you made fun of him, he'd laugh heartily with you. Some felt a need to defend him: 'You're a nice guy, Théoneste, but a bit simple. If only you were a little smarter, your life would be much better.' 'But I have no desire to be a clever person,' he'd reply while spitting out his wad of tobacco. 'There's a need for people like me. A village without an idiot is a village without a future.'

That would make the Italian woman laugh. She thought that, all in all, of all the residents of Nyamata, my father was the one with the most common sense. She took him seriously, even if, like everyone else, she'd have to deride him from time to time for his terrible bouts of drunkenness. One fine day, she had gotten out of a dusty Land Rover that then left immediately, as if this were the land of lepers. As she got out of the car, she told all the curious assembled around her, 'You'll have plenty of time to examine me! I've come here to live. For now, I want to find some place where I can leave my luggage.'

Then she disappeared into the church to talk to Father Manolo. He led her to the house near our concession; I've always seen her live there until that ill-fated day when she was hacked to pieces on the gravel path in front of the church. Little did she know that she had left her native Italy only to die among us. Although it wasn't clear why she was here. To those who asked her, she simply replied that she had heard about our hills and our lakes. And she could always make herself useful to those who were interested. She could teach reading and writing to those who hadn't had a chance to go to school, give sewing and embroidery lessons and introduce the bored young ones to gardening and chicken and hog farming. But, as my father used to say, 'in Nyamata, there are only lazybones and liars, or maybe it's the other way around.' After the first three trial weeks, only a dozen at the most stayed with her. The others went back to the Fraternité Bar to drown their boredom in alcohol and checkers. Like my father, she liked the smell of grass, the simple life, and work well done. She'd go to him at any time of the day to ask him the best way to dig up yams or to fix this delicious dish made with sorghum seeds we call *impegeri*. She was at home at our house and we felt comfortable at hers. Like us, she believed that there's dignity in working the soil and living is not shameful. But there are those who are bothered by that, who are never so happy as when they're harassing other people. A crazy rumor began to spread: machetes had been imported from China and grenades from France. Thousands of people were being dragged into the hills. A bloodbath more dreadful than the previous ones was going to descend on the village. 'Tall tales,' my father would roar. 'Nothing will happen. They'll never dare. Flee if you wish, but no threats will keep me from taking care of my field.' The Brazilian mother superior agreed with him: 'The sisters and I spent the night in prayers,' she'd repeat. 'Tomorrow, the Belgian priests will say Mass. Act natural. If something is going to take place, it'll stop at Kanzenzé. Like the last times, it won't go past the bridge.' The Italian woman didn't say anything. But it was obvious she was grim, tortured by some unknown worries. From the top of the avocado tree that I liked to climb to pick fruits, I enjoyed watching her working in her vegetable garden. She'd suddenly straighten up, as if seized by stomach pains, drop her hoe, wipe her hands on her overalls, and for a long time gaze toward the hills.

Some saw her as a good woman, others as a madwoman. Evidently you had to be one or the other, and more plausibly both, to go in the middle of the night and wake up the judge and the *sous-préfet*, grab on to their pajamas, and scream at them that something had to be done before it was too late. When she saw that wasn't working, she spent the next days glued to her telephone. And so her voice was heard on all international radios. She was asking that the *Watican* and the *United Notions* be alerted. A great tragedy was about to happen. Tutsis were going to be killed, Hutus who weren't for President Habyarimana were going to be killed, everything that moves was going to be killed, if nothing was done. The *sous-préfet* came in person to knock on her door. I was in the vegetable garden and heard everything: 'You're a foreigner,' he said. 'Don't meddle in our affairs.' He talked about many other things too complicated for my age. All I understood was that the matter was serious because he threatened to make her be quiet and left slamming the door.

I was getting ready to go to school when they arrived. Some were armed with clubs, others with machetes. I don't know what came over her but she couldn't find anything better to do than to go outside to look. They grabbed her on her doorstep. They hit her on the back of the head. They dragged her to the church. They hacked her to pieces.

★ ★

Contrary to what we might think, it's not easy to kill a man. I think Musinkôro's body was still moving. It took the last bullet to put an end to his whole soul. What a racket something as little as a mere revolver can make. The whole world seemed to have gathered around me to fret and weep. The shots must have roused half the town. I could hear doors slamming, sleepy voices calling out: had the sky fallen, was it the beginning of another bloodbath? For a few seconds, the gun still in my hand, I froze in front of the corpse. Oddly enough, no one thought of hog-tying me or lynching me. When daylight returned inside my head, my first reflex was to look out the window. Luckily that day there were no wood panels, no scraps of slate or cardboard pieces obstructing it. I took a running jump and fell among the pumpkins growing around the avocado tree. I took off through the cornfields and the small courtyards cluttered with bricks and coals. I ran the rest of the night, probably returning to the same place several times, before collapsing in a manioc field. In the light of dawn, I realized that I was in front of the old tin mine near the City of Blue Angels. I hadn't planned it, but some animal survival instinct had brought me there. 'Animals remember the dens where they grew up,' old Funga used to say. I hadn't literally grown up there, but I knew that not only was it difficult to spot but it was also riddled with tunnels where it was dry, and it was located right next to the dining hall. I imagined myself surviving on the interns' leftovers. I had to resign myself to swallowing my disappointment: the plates were piled up in a corner of the kitchen clean as a freshly peeled onion; besides banana and manioc skins, the garbage cans contained a crusty end of bread that I tried unsuccessfully to grind with a stone. I remembered the manioc groves and patches of banana trees nearby.

I didn't last more than a week. I didn't mind the brown rats, the moles, the rainfall. It was the torrential bouts of diarrhea caused by the green bananas and the manioc shoots (that tasted like aloe), and especially the unbearable desire to smoke that made me come out of my hole. I waited until the sun had slipped halfway down behind Mount Kigali to crawl toward the brush. I picked up an abandoned hoe and put it over my shoulder. Now I looked like a carefree ordinary farmer returning from his field. Walking was going to do me good. I was less than five kilometers from the outskirts of Kigali. All I had to do was climb over the thickets along the road then melt into the crowd of traders and porters swarming through the back streets of the shanty towns and the sidewalks of the main thoroughfares. Night was falling when I reached the edges of the market. I had lost my gun but not my dollars. I slipped into a poorly lit corner and called a *busenessman* over. I traded only twenty dollars; now was not the time to play the *nouveau riche*. Besides a piece of smoked meat, I bought cigarettes, bread, and cookies. It was child's play to go back to my lair. Cops are big oafs; they see only what you show them.

I ate with relish and quickly became drowsy. I heard what I thought was a human voice. I rose up partly so I could listen better. It must have been the call of a Barbary ape, distorted by echo. I lay back down but I had to sit up again a few seconds later. There was no doubt about it: someone was calling me.

'Faustin, wake up! Faustin, don't be afraid. It's me, Tatien. Let me in and please don't shoot.'

I tiptoed toward the opening. I climbed midway up the old iron stairs so I could scrutinize the outside. I caught sight of a shadow seated on the ground right outside the hole. All around, all I could see were the rock formations and the outline of the acacias.

'Okay, I'll risk it. Come down if you want, but hands up in the air. The slightest threatening gesture and I shoot. In case you're not alone, your friends should know that I won't miss you before they kill me.'

It really was Tatien. He had recognized me at the market and followed me from a distance.

'We're all being watched. They think we know where you're hiding.

Coming here, so near, was a great idea! Everyone thinks you're in Tanzania. . . . Say something. Don't play the tough guy. As far as I'm concerned, you're not a murderer. To me, you're just Faustin. You don't believe me? They chased everyone out before closing HQ. Now it's everyone for himself. We barely say hello when we meet in the street. You have to admit it was quite a shock. . . . You want news of your brother and sisters, I suppose? Well, I don't have any.'

I wasn't playing the tough guy. I couldn't answer. I hadn't been here long but already I wasn't used to people. In a way, I wanted to chase him out, in another, I felt sorry for him. He had traveled all this way for me. I owed him something. I racked my brain. All I could say was, 'You're sure no one followed you?'

'You'd already be under siege.'

'That's true.'

'You know, you don't need to take risks. I can take care of your supplies. I'll come at night. I don't mind the walk.'

That was a terrific idea.

I gave him half of my money for the essentials and I added a one-hundred-dollar bill.

'That's the price of your silence!'

'You plan to end your days here?'

'Go! Do as we planned, and before you do something stupid, re-member my gun.'

(Until the end, he thought I still had one.)

First he brought me a blanket, then an old moss mattress, and even a pillow and some patched clothes. Since I couldn't wash, at least I could change rags. Now I'd eat a piece of yam for lunch and a can of sardines for dinner. I got a pack of cigarettes every other day or so and sometimes even some beer. Three months went by. You don't have to believe me, but life as a wild animal isn't so bad. The world of refined men and I were now an ocean apart. I was comfortable in my hole. I didn't need the outside world. My parents, my sisters, my brother? Their memory had deserted my head all on its own. I regretted nothing, I felt no blame. I didn't need any other place: neither Kigali, nor Tanzania, nor this green paradise in the Psalms that Father Manolo had so often promised. I had blotted out the world and believed that in return the world had done the same with me.

That morning I was awakened by dogs barking and footsteps on the gravel and the couch grass. Besides the cries of the City of Blue Angels boarders, sometimes I'd hear groups of poachers walking very close to the mine talking low about their hunting trophies and their sexual conquests. There was nothing to worry about. I had become a ghost or a creature from outer space. Bullets from the living don't hit ghosts.

The piercing sound of the whistles made me put my fingers in my ears. There must have been twenty of them running in all directions through the galleries. A flashlight shined in my face. I was picked up by the feet and the hands. Outside, fifty others were waiting, machine guns aimed at the mine. Tatien was among them. He let his arms drop in a gesture of sorrow while mine were being tied.

'You have to understand, I couldn't keep the secret anymore.'

*   *

The third time Claudine visited me Monsieur Bukuru, who had arrived before her, was shut away with the warden in his office. We had to wait in the hall. I had never seen her with earrings before. She looked like a Boganda princess. The comings and goings of the prisoners in the hall would sometimes surge against us and propel me into her. I'd maneuver to pin her against the door so I could make the most of her perfume and the provocative figure magnificently accentuated by the tailored blouse and the skintight pants she was wearing that day. I'll always regret not taking her in my arms and declaring my love to her that instant. She would have slapped me and called me crazy, but at least I would have kissed her.

'I spoke with the warden,' Monsieur Bukuru told me. 'I got him to let you have outside visiting privileges. But there's a snag and that's why our meeting lasted so long. You must realize that you have no family in Kigali.'

'He can come to my house!'

'The law is firm, Mademoiselle Karemera: outside visits are not permitted unless there's a direct relative. Do you have a blood relationship with this . . . I mean, this young man?'

'No.'

'You see.'

'I could say I'm his cousin.'

78

'Only the father, the mother, the brothers, and the sisters. That's the law. Now, if you'll excuse me, I have another client. You can tell him yourself what I told you on the phone.'

'I suppose this is about me.'

'Who else are we going to talk about, Faustin? If the two of us are here, it's for you. I beg you, make my task easier instead of annoying everyone.'

'Forget it, Mademoiselle Karemera. I'll keep defending this renegade since I gave my word. But I'll tell you, I would have done better to break my leg.'

'No one insults me!' I shouted. 'Not even my father, Théoneste, ever did. And, as far as I know, you're not my father, moron!'

'Faustin,' sobbed Claudine. 'I forbid you . . .'

'You talk about me as if I were a package. First, why don't you start by asking me if I want to get out of here! . . . Claudine, don't you think I deserve better as a lawyer?'

I hadn't realized it, but I was now standing menacingly in front of this crook. I rushed toward him. I was ready to bite. Claudine, beside herself, managed to drag me toward the door while old Bukuru stamped his feet as he nervously readjusted his tie.

'Can you imagine?' she asked me. 'What if the warden had seen you? What if the jabirus had heard you? Your trial is tomorrow at 2:00 P.M.. If you act like that, not even God will be able to help you.'

I received the news with the same interest as if she had said, 'Tomorrow, at 2:00 P.M., it'll rain on Nyamirambo stadium.' My future – if perchance I still had one – I didn't give a damn about it. But my body was driving me crazy. I rose on my tiptoes, kissed her on both cheeks, and fled like a thief.

★   ★

I was taken from the Juniors' Club in handcuffs. It was raining. But that's not all that made me belligerent. We had spent the night getting high on hashish and glue while weighing my fate.

'Don't worry,' said Misago, 'if they sentence you to death, you'll be executed in spectacular fashion at Nyamirambo stadium with a bunch of big shots. There would be lots of guys to clap and girls to weep. You'd be leaving this world a well-known person.'

'He's not that important,' replied Matata. 'Nyamirambo stadium, that's for the *génocidaires*. He's killed only one man, if that.'

'Shut up, idiots!' growled Ayirwanda. 'It's not just anyone they sentence to death, especially not a minor.'

'Meaning?'

'A minor? Well, that's a little bit of a man like you who shows off like an elephant but who still reeks of his mother's milk.'

They all died laughing pointing a finger at me. In their eyes, I must have been less than a tick, less than a goat turd. We had reached that drug-induced state when the line separating euphoria from the desire to kill is no longer clear. I rushed toward Ayirwanda holding a piece of glass in my hand.

'Well, let them sentence me to death! That way I can kill you all, and you first, Ayirwanda! In my case, it wouldn't change anything; for you, everything would be different.'

'Don't listen to him, Ayirwanda,' said Matata. 'Worst case, he'll be sentenced to empty the slop pail. And of course that would be dandy for us, right?'

They must have still been chortling demonically when I fell asleep. I woke up with all the night sounds heard around the pond in Ngenda in my head and a disgusting taste of shit and ash on my tongue. The jabirus got me out of there before I had time to swallow the dishwater without sugar and bread they serve us as breakfast. My head was bobbing and I was talking to myself in the paddy wagon. I had to wait a long time in an adjoining room. Claudine managed to find me there and to talk to me in spite of the presence of the jabirus.

'You're all right?'

'Sure, I'm fine!'

'You sure, Faustin?'

'What makes you doubt it?'

'I don't doubt it, I'm just worried. Right now there are plenty of reasons for me to worry about you.'

'If you're really worried about me, then . . .'

I wanted to say: 'Then, love me once and for all. Lift your wrapper and squat on my legs. Let's do what is required in such cases and let the jabirus croak with resentment and jealousy. After that, they can hang me if they want or throw me from the rock of Kagera!' But a remnant of decency sprang from my conscience and I couldn't continue. You don't become loony from a single impulse.

'Then what?' she continued as she removed snot from the corner of my nostril.

She seemed quite short of breath. Some ugly circles – the first ones since I knew her – adorned her eyes, and her bracelets jingled on her trembling wrist.

'Then you think I've gone mad because of what happened yesterday?'

She repeated several times, 'What happened yesterday, just what happened yesterday, Faustin?'

I was no longer paying attention to what she was saying. Her voice was blending in with those of the jabirus chattering about their favorite subjects: the changing of the guards that never happened on time and the unforeseen fights among the prisoners . . . I wanted to cry in the hollow of her neck and whisper in her ear, 'Then, take care of yourself instead.' But as I've already said, my eye sockets are now empty; I have no tears left. That's how it is.

Old Bukuru arrived midmorning. He kissed Claudine several times and felt the need to become considerate.

'Well, little man, I hope you're in a nicer mood now. It would be better that way. Today is the big day. If you can restrain yourself, it'll all go well. The judges aren't any meaner than other people. You'll see, I'll get you out of this if you show some goodwill. I've rescued many a head and in cases much more complicated than yours.'

He put his attaché case down, sat on a bench, and talked with Claudine as if I weren't there. This is what I heard.

'I'm glad that he's first. It'll be good training for the rest. I have no fewer than five cases during the day.'

'You'll have to excuse him! It's not that he's so bad but you have to understand what he's been through.'

'Oh, you social workers, you see victims everywhere. I find justice much more humane than pity. Yet, believe me, I'm no persecutor.'

They were whispering, but I had no trouble following. 'The rabbit's ears are very long and they get even longer as the wild beasts are approaching,' Théoneste, my father, used to say.

Bukuru lit a cigar. Claudine asked him, 'How are you going to counterattack?'

'Well, first, I'll bring up his young age, although I hate resorting to pity. After all, he is a minor even if the law isn't very clear on that. In fact, there's no more real law. There's nothing authentic left. We're on the threshold of a new life. The whole thing needs to be redone: history, geography, government, customs, so why not the way we understand children?'

'For the prosecutor, Kirikumaso, an underage *génocidaire* is a *génocidaire* like any other.'

'Just let poor Kirikumaso rant on. This child is not a *génocidaire*; he simply avenged his sister. Crime of passion, family honor! . . . It's funny, there aren't many families left, yet we insist on defending their honor anyway. Just because there's been a genocide, it doesn't mean Rwandans have lost all moral sense.'

We were led through winding hallways cluttered with old benches and talkative secretaries. We entered a large room full of armed jabirus, women carrying their children on their backs, and itinerant merchants with their sticks of chewing gum and their wristwatch displays. Someone shouted an order and everyone stood up. Men dressed like women entered. 'They're the judges,' Claudine whispered to me. Each one took out of his bag a pile of papers two or three meters high. They talked until midmorning. Half of the people in the room had fallen asleep when Bukuru finally answered. That's when one of them turned toward me.

'Tell us, Faustin Nsenghimana, why did you buy this gun?'

'You know very well: everyone in town has one.'

'We're not talking about the whole town, we're talking about you, Faustin Nsenghimana.'

'Were you already planning to kill Musinkôro?' asked a second one. 'You must have had a disagreement at this Rutongo camp?'

'Yes . . .'

'Good! So you already wanted to kill him?'

'No!'

'My client is too young,' Bukuru said. 'He can't grasp all the nuances of your questions. So, please . . .'

'Too young to understand our questions but old enough to get a gun,' bellowed a third one. 'You must realize, sir, this individual killed a man.'

'Faustin,' insisted the very first one, 'if I understood correctly, you killed this man because you found him, let's say, with your sister?'

'You, if I slept with your sister, you'd do what I did to this swine, wouldn't you? Family honor isn't debatable anywhere in the world, at least not with the Nsenghimanas.'

Some people were laughing, others were applauding. Bukuru was nervously yanking on my shirt and gesturing madly. And Claudine's face was beaded with perspiration; she was on the verge of fainting. On the other hand, I was pretty proud of myself.

'You're on trial, Faustin, not the rest of the world,' the third one said choking with rage.

'Tell me, Faustin,' continued the second judge, 'at this famous HQ, you weren't all little saints, if we're to believe Tatien. You slept with some of the girls there, I mean other people's sisters, and no one, as far as I know, planted a bullet in your belly.'

'That's just it, they were other people's sisters.'

More and more people were crowding into the room as I talked. No one was interested in the judges, or the jabirus standing guard, or the woman with the blond wig typing on a typewriter while sniffling like a bush pig. The laughter and the admiring glances were for me. With all due respect to this idiot Matata, I didn't need Nyamirambo stadium any more to establish my renown.

'Faustin Nsenghimana,' threatened the first judge, 'here, you're in court! We're your elders and your judges! Be polite or we're going to find you in contempt of court.'

'I've been rotting in a rat hole for two years. If you think there's a worse sentence than that, then go ahead and sentence me! As my father, Théoneste, used to say, "The one-eyed man is closer to the blind man than to healthy people."'

'Do you regret your deed?' the third judge asked me.

'I'm sorry, sir, that I have not an ounce of regret.'

Amid the growing clamor in the crowd, I heard a voice saying, 'That's one who knows how to defend himself. The little guy's not afraid to speak up for himself.'

The first judge pounded his gavel stirring up dust on his desk.

'Silence, or I'll clear the room!'

'But he should be careful if he wants to save his neck,' advised an old woman on the first bench on my right as she picked her teeth, not taking notice of the warning.

'Heh, my good woman,' I replied, 'that's all I've done these past few years is save my neck. If I get my head cut off, I'll regret only one thing, that I didn't take more advantage of the good times.'

'Oh,' said the first judge, 'you do manage to regret sometimes!

Your own life, of course, but surely not that of your victim. You're a monster, Faustin! You don't deserve to be part of the human race.'

'I've never thought that belonging to the human race was praise-worthy. I've never been as happy as when I was in the tin mine.'

'You tell us that you would regret not having lived more. What does that mean to you, living?'

'Eating a good dish of umushagoro, getting drunk when you please, and screwing the woman you love without the law meddling.'

Up until then, the crowd had been on my side. Now it was quiet. That was very painful. I could feel it on my shoulders like a load of burning wood or ice. I was well aware that things were getting serious but I was too far gone in my euphoria to turn back.

'What!' I said looking at the dumbfounded crowd and the haggard looks on the judges' faces. 'You're not going to tell me that you've never gotten a beautiful woman in the sack. Unless . . .'

Now no one was laughing. The terrifying voice of the first judge made the windows rattle. In comparison, the sound of thunder would have seemed like water lapping.

'Get this scum out of here before I lose control!'

My head banged against the benches and the walls. In vain I looked for Claudine's face before I ended up outside, head over heels, my knees like porridge. She probably left to avoid dying of shame.

It was only the next day when I saw tough Ayirwanda in tears that I understood.

I had just been sentenced to death.

★   ★

As a little boy I loathed anything that seemed mysterious. Predictions worried me. I was terrified of the dark. Nothing reassured me more than the light of day when I was certain the ground held firm under my feet and the sky was still up there; that a monkey on a grévéhia tree limb wasn't some goblin and that the movement in a pyrethrum thicket was a moorhen and nothing more. I resented old Funga for interpreting any old lightning strike as a sign of threat from the heavens and I resented Father Manolo for so often invoking this Christian god, so quick to fry you for all eternity for a mere sin of gluttony. To control my anxiety, I'd tell myself that none of this was true, that they invented stories to amuse the white beards and scare the children. However, when I saw on the Fraternité Bar TV Father Manolo collapse at the pope's feet in the Kabwayi Church and I heard the farmers whisper about another bloodbath coming, I panicked. I ran to my father, Théoneste, who was working in the banana grove.

'Father Théoneste, tell me, am I a Hutu?'

'A genuine one since I'm a Hutu.'

It was a relief to hear that. I wanted to make absolutely certain.

'So I'm not a Tutsi!'

'Oh yes, you are, since your mother, Axelle, is a Tutsi . . . But why are you asking me this?'

'It's good to know who you are, right? Especially in these times.'

'That's for sure, son. But go on and snare birds, don't listen to these idiots from Kigali. All they know is how to tell lies on the radio. Hutu, Tutsi, that doesn't mean much; you might as well compare water with water. Your mother Axelle was the prettiest shepherdess in the village of Bimirura. Five suitors brought a goat to her father. Well, I'm the one who got her hand.'

From there, I rushed over to see the Brazilian nuns.

'Here I am, Mother Superior,' I said as I crossed the threshold. 'Do you want me to trim your rose bushes?'

'That would be so nice, sweet young Faustin. Just this morning I was telling the sisters that they needed clipping. We never have a free moment to devote to these poor roses: housework, sewing, candies, catechesis . . . You'll be rewarded in heaven, young Faustin. God is always magnanimous toward helpful souls.'

I trimmed the roses, swept the porch, brought in all the clothes drying outside.

'Mother Superior, since God is magnanimous, do you think He'll be willing to protect me when the killings start?' I asked before leaving.

'What killings? He'll protect us all! There, take this,' – she stuffed my pockets with enough candies for a whole week, plus some cookies and goat cheese – 'and stop worrying. Nothing will happen to Faustin, and me either for that matter. Only, don't forget to help your old father and to pray to the Lord even when no one's watching you.'

I went home whistling and got an old game out to play with Donatienne. Funga chose that instant to burst into our house.

'Théoneste, have you heard what's going on?'

'No!' my father answered.

'Théoneste, you'll always be more stupid than others. They shot down the president's plane and you don't even know it!'

* *

Matata scratched a bit of match, lit a piece of rag, and walked over to me, his eyes gleaming with mischief.

'What are you doing, you big goof?' asked Ayirwanda, who was still drying his tears.

'I wanted to see up close the face of a man condemned to die. I thought it would look horrifying. But it doesn't; it looks just like all the others with monkey eyebrows and nostril hair.'

No one was amused. You don't laugh during a wake. Since my return from court, everyone has been pampering me. The jabirus give me cigarettes. Ayirwanda sees to my supply of hashish and glue. Leftover yams and bread crusts reach me through the long human chain separating me from the other cells. I've already told you, there's nothing more sacred than a dying man. The real enemy is the man bursting with health; he's the one we take our aggressions out on. That's how it is. In the faces around me I read devotion as well as sadness. You bet. My new circumstances earned me admiration and even – I didn't expect that much – jealousy. And it's true, I'm not to be pitied. All men nearing death meditate over the important moments of their existence, and when I do, not a trace of unhappiness comes to mind. Fifteen years of life on earth and, in the end, nothing to regret. Except maybe Claudine, her smile and her breasts, her perfume, her marvelous little ass. But I've learned to do without Claudine even. Once we're on the brink of the grave, the play is over. The only thing left to do is let the curtain fall. All it takes is a little lucidity to appreciate the farce, and there's nothing more lucid than a man who's about to croak. My old father, Théoneste, wasn't all that stupid, he was just lucid. I remember what he told Corporal Nyumurowo when he grabbed my kite out of my hands: 'So you think that's the enemy you need to destroy? It's obvious you don't understand the words of the ancients. "If you hate a man, let him live!" That's what the ancients used to say.'

* *

86

So the president's plane was shot down on the sixth. As it fell from the sky, it brought down with it a shower of bad omens. We saw a herd of topis running through the village, asps and chameleons coming out of everywhere, and, in broad daylight, a flight of owls perched on the church roof. Flasks of palm wine filled up with blood and rows of ants invaded homes and wells. 'So!' cursed Théoneste, my father. 'In 1972 also, we saw a tide of frogs covering the schoolyard and even a couple of albinos from who knows where romping under the grévéhias. The fact remains that, again that year, the killings didn't go beyond Nyabarongo Bridge. This is Nyamata!' People thought he had become a seer because nothing happened the next day. However, on the twelfth, the first survivors covered with wounds arrived to ask for refuge and, between comas and death rattles, told us what was going on in Rutongo or in Kanzenzé. The impaling of pregnant women and the carving up of the dying. I reacted with the same happiness I felt on dark nights when I'd imagine the miseries of a child abandoned in the forest, trembling with cold, threatened by wolves and hyenas, while I was warm and under the jovial protection of Théoneste, my father. Here nothing was happening yet. The village went on hoeing the potato plots, playing igisoro, and getting drunk on banana beer and palm wine. In the evening, we'd gather round the Fraternité Bar TV and Mille Collines radio. We'd watch the fellows on TV explaining how to handle a machete. We'd hear war songs. It was sort of fun. What's happening far away can't be totally tragic. Someone among us even exclaimed, 'That one,' (he was referring to the TV guy wearing a raffia hat), 'I'd never hire him for my banana harvest: he's holding his machete by the blade!' And of course, everyone laughed. Was it my father's steadfast optimism or the mother superior's prayers? The village was learning to laugh again. A cautious optimism had succeeded the mad anxiety of the previous few weeks. In fact we saw people who had fled return from the bush. The gods had spared us five times in a row, so why wouldn't they do it again this time?

⋆ ⋆

On the thirteenth at dawn, for the first time, jeeps and trucks loaded with Interharamwe militias, high and drunk, crossed the Nyabarongo bridge. They emerged in the alleys of Nyamata amid shouting and horn blowing. The men jumped down from the vehicles and fired in the air. They rolled around in the schoolyard singing mournful chants that terrified even the witch doctor, Funga. They sacked the Oprovia store, broke the windows at the Prudence drugstore, and emptied bottles at the Fraternité Bar. After that, they rushed toward the church, took turns relieving themselves on the Italian woman's grave, then threatened to burn the church down.

'What are we going to do today?' shouted their main leader.

'We're going to burn the Tutsis and their friends!'

'Why are we going to do that?'

'Because they're cockroaches!'

They chanted this as they paraded past the courthouse, beneath the town hall kapok trees and on the soccer field. Then, when the sun was high as the church steeple, they climbed back into their vehicles and cleared out still shouting.

Everyone had been content just to observe from their doorsteps or lying low in a thicket, not daring to breathe too loud or sneeze. When they had all left, we gathered in the churchyard as if by plan. To feel less afraid, each person needed to be near another.

'Those are some strange little jokers,' exulted my father. 'Maybe there's nothing going on anywhere and they just want to show off. Come on, let's return to our fields. And next time, let's not waste our time for so little. I've already told you: this is Nyamata.'

'So the wounded who showed up here must be some really good little jokers,' sniggered someone dryly.

At that moment the Brazilian mother superior came out of the vegetable garden pushing a wheelbarrow full of lettuce and artichokes.

'You see, good old Théoneste is the most sensible one among you. Come on, do as he says, go back to your work. Avoid forming large groups; that's the sort of thing that stirs them up. Nothing's going to happen. At least . . . if you continue praying. You bunch of heathens remember Christ only when death is hot on your heels. Oh, one would almost wish for moments like these: there have never been so many people in church.'

★ ★

The night of the fourteenth, the Belgian priests fled toward Burundi.

The fifteenth, we got up at dawn as usual. My father and I were washing our faces at the well before a breakfast of sorghum gruel. Old Funga showed up, creeping like a thief through the *lougan* of manioc plants.[14]

'You intrigue me, Funga,' shouted my father. 'What are you up to? Did the spirits forbid you to use the road like everyone else?'

'I can tell you, Théoneste. You're not very clever but, thank goodness for us, you're not indiscreet either. Here goes: I'm off to the Ntarama marsh.'

'And what are you going to do at the Ntarama marsh so early?'

'I'm going to throw away my charms. I don't believe in the future anymore.'

'Throw away your charms! Now that needs to be said several times before I'll believe it.'

'You just have to follow me to see what I'm going to do.'

'Oh, no. I have my sorghum to harvest and my nanny goats to look after. You see, Funga, I've decided to mind my own business and close my eyes to the dramatics I see around me. Sometimes I have the impression people have gone mad.'

'Not people, Théoneste, the gods. The gods have gone mad. At times I've suspected as much. But, since last night, I now know what to make of things.'

'What happened?'

'Don't ask me that. The gods created the world in the utmost secrecy; to tell all is forbidden. You should be glad you don't know what I know.'

He started to sniffle rapidly; I thought he was going to start crying. He adjusted the pouch slung over his shoulder and kicked up some grass with his rattan cane. He chanted some idiocies and dove into the bush.

'Let's go eat our gruel,' my father said. 'He's gone mad, that's true. But not even mad people go so far as to throw away their books of magic. You'll see, he won't do it.'

As if to prove him right, Funga rushed back noisily parting the tall grass. He sat down for a moment on the edge of the well, unable to hide his extreme distress.

'If you outlive me, Théoneste, remember to put this rock of Kagera

14. *Lougan* is the Franco-Senegalese word for plot of land; the word has been used since the eighteenth century. – Trans.

89

back in its right place. Otherwise there's much to fear, and not just for the village, but for the whole world. Strange things are parading behind my eyes: hybrid beings, mountains of eyeless heads being carried along on rivers of blood. Oh, it's the fault of the older generation like us. We've been neglecting the gods lately. We served the god of others. We shall pay!'

That blew a hole in my father's legendary optimism.

'Here,' he told me as he was putting the gourd of gruel down on the gravel. 'Take two good helpings; you never know if you'll have some tomorrow.'

For the first time he forgot to don his old straw hat before going off to the fields. That worried my mother when she found out. At first she thought I should take it out to him but on second thought she changed her mind.

'Instead, you and the girls go play with the kite while I see to the preparations. The mother superior is due here very soon. Once she's picked up her milk, we'll join him to help him pick beans and we'll take his hat to him at the same time.'

She had barely finished saying that when, his face contorted by anger, my father appeared.

'Isn't there anyone in this house to remind me I forgot my hat?'

'Some hat!' my mother replied angrily. 'If it were up to me this rag would have already been thrown in the fire. As if we weren't already ashamed of you.'

'Don't you provoke me, Axelle, this isn't my best day.'

'Your best day. Why don't you tell other people? If you knew how they see you. I'm the only one you act important with.'

'You're not supposed to talk to a husband that way, especially during such times. Be quiet and hand me the flask of palm wine before I explode.'

There were scenes like that five or six times a day at our house. It never got too serious. For us kids, it was a great opportunity to have a good laugh. Our parents were never so funny as when they were about to have a row. But my father started to calm down under the effects of the palm wine. He was singing at the top of his voice when the mother superior's cart came bouncing over the gravel in the road.

'You sure don't seem worried,' she told him when she set foot in our yard.

He helped her boy load the milk cans without interrupting his same old songs.

'Why don't you take a little rancid butter before you leave, Mother Superior.'

'No, Théoneste. But if you happen to go to the bush, don't forget to bring me back some aloe roots. I need to purge two of my young boarders who have tapeworms.'

'That's what I like about you, Mother Superior: you are as unshakable as I am. Just think, in the village there are people who don't even bother to pick their coffee beans on the pretext that they won't be around to reap the profits. Can you imagine?'

The mother superior straightened her cape and motioned to the boy. She was on her way to the vegetable garden, but she jumped and turned around without telling the servant who was near the church with his milk cart.

'Did you forget something, Mother Superior?' my father asked. 'The rancid butter maybe? I was wondering. No one turns down my wife Axelle's rancid butter.'

'Let me have the little girls. They'll help me shell beans.'

'Then they'll have to take Ambroise with them,' insisted my mother. 'If he's left alone, all he does is cry and I won't be able to finish my housework.'

'Er . . . When I said the little girls . . . I meant Ambroise too,' mumbled the mother superior.

She took the children and disappeared. That was the last time I saw her.

★ ★

Once he had emptied his first wine flask of the day, my father asked for another. My mother, who was as passive as a slug, could sometimes get strict: it was no! He resigned himself to taking his hat and his gardening tools and going back to his field.

'We're going with you,' my mother suggested. 'I'll do my housework later.'

'No. Join me midmorning. There's too much dew right now. I'm going to work on this old bird trap while I wait for things to dry a little.'

I was going to be able to enjoy my kite in peace. My brother and my sisters wouldn't ask me to lend it to them or show them how it works. My father wouldn't bug me asking for his flask or sending me to the other end of the village to get some batteries for his radio or some chewing tobacco. I put on my sneakers (the Italian woman had brought them back from Kigali for me a few weeks before she was murdered). The wind was blowing hard. My kite was flying on its own, as majestic as an eagle soaring over the trees. I made a few runs between the church and the Brazilian nuns' convent before setting off on a long journey through the village. Everything seemed quiet for the moment. However I noticed that some houses were marked by a large cross in red chalk. The market was empty and the doors of the Fraternité Bar were shut tight. Under the mango trees and in front of the service station, a few small groups had formed. The few people I met cried in astonishment.

'Oh, that's Théoneste's son. Look at him playing with his kite! The killings are about to start and he's playing with his kite. There's no doubt about it, idiots are born to be happy.'

Lizende, the son of Gicari the tailor, caught up with me in front of the beauty salon.

'We're all going to die, Faustin, and you're playing with your kite. Why taunt death, Faustin?'

'The mother superior and my father have claimed nothing will cross the bridge. If you'd listened to them, you wouldn't be in this state.'

'Poor Faustin! As I speak right now, they're slaughtering the village of Ntarama, which means they've definitely crossed the bridge.'

'I don't believe you.'

'Go inside any hut, ask the crying women. Ask the men holed up in the latrines and the attics. No one has been able to flee; the village is surrounded.'

'It all seems quiet here.'

'People are resigned. What else do you want them to do?'

He showed me the percale fabric he was holding under his arm.

'Look, that's my shroud. My father, Gicari, gave one to each member of the family. We're all Tutsis at home, one hundred percent Tutsi. These people are real animals; they know how to kill but they don't know how to bury. Dying with the shroud in your hand is as good as being buried. That's what my father told us.'

He reminded me of Father Manolo evoking the last judgment with terrifying eyes and in a resonant voice that seemed to come from a mouth other than his. This time, I was really scared. And for me, fear always settles in the bladder. I handed him my kite and went over to a ditch to have a long pee. As I was fastening my pants, I heard a racket coming from the road to Kigali, then a detonation. Thick smoke was rising from the power station. It must have been the signal. The peaceful small groups I had seen earlier under the mango trees and in front of the service station jumped up in the air brandishing hammers, machetes, and studded clubs while vehicles of militias were entering the village. It was the same scenario as the time before except that, this time, it was for real. I now understood the meaning of the red crosses on the walls: those were Tutsi houses. Some of them on fire, others were surrounded. Women were trying to save their kids. They were quickly caught. They were made to lie down in their own yards and their tendons were slit. Their children's heads were smashed against the walls.

'You see, I wasn't lying,' shouted Lizende, almost glad to be right.

He was still standing in the middle of the road, the kite string still wrapped around his hand. I had to pry his fingers open myself to take it from him. His body was motionless and cold. Although he was still standing, I thought he was dead. I touched his chest and called out his name several times.

'Lizende! Lizende!'

He didn't answer. His eyes were turned toward his father's shop, whose red cross was perfectly visible from the two hundred meters away where we were standing. Chanting their war cries, men armed with machetes were on their way to it. He began to talk to himself and walked straight toward the shop. He must have gone mad. I wanted to cry out, to catch up with him. I did nothing of the kind. A totally different thought was haunting me: what had happened to my parents? I rushed toward our house, convinced they were dead. No, they were really alive, seated on the edge of the well, my mother in tears and my father clumsily trying to console her.

'I thought . . .'

'You thought we were dead,' my father cut in. 'No, it's the Gisimanas lying among their cattle. You know, the cattle keepers whose pen is at the other end of my field. Some people came out of the ferns to slice them up as soon as this horrible detonation sounded. So I rushed over here to see if anything had happened to you. The Gisimanas were RPF sympathizers. But we've never been part of anything. Nothing will happen to us. All we have to do is stay here.

'My children,' moaned my mother. 'They're going to kill my children!'

'Your children are with the white woman. Who'll dare touch a white woman?'

I sat down too, with my kite still in my hand. My brother, my sisters, I hadn't even thought about them. I wanted to throw myself in my father's arms to thank him for his solid good sense. Of course, they'd never dare take them from the Brazilian nuns' convent!

'So, may I? Just one sip, just one! You must see that I really need some, especially now.'

'Take all the flasks left and drink until you're falling down drunk. My children are going to be killed and you think about getting drunk.'

In such cases, he always felt a little ashamed but still he would end up in the attic where the palm wine was kept. This time, he didn't have time; a voice crackling in a loudspeaker made all three of us jump.

'This is your *sous-préfet*! This is your *sous-préfet*! Everyone must meet at the church. The army will protect us. I repeat: the army will protect us.'

⋆　⋆

Outside, sure enough, soldiers were jumping out of trucks and jeeps and lining up along the fence surrounding the cowsheds, around the church as well as on the Italian woman's veranda. Dazed people were coming out of everywhere to converge on the church. Some were carrying the wounded or unconscious women, others, just their belongings. The church was already full to bursting; we had great difficulty finding a place. Those coming after us were directed toward the town hall, the courthouse, the school or the soccer field.

The loudspeaker crackled once more.

'Are there any Hutus among you? The Hutus are asked to leave. I repeat, the Hutus are asked to leave with their identity cards in hand.'

Some one hundred people rushed toward the exit. That made a little more room even if it was still difficult to breathe comfortably; the little bit of air reaching us stank of fresh paint and unwashed bodies. Corporal Nyumurow, brandishing his rifle, made his way toward us.

'Well, Théoneste, what are you waiting for?'

'My friend, you mean that we can go?'

'You can leave! You're Hutu aren't you?'

'Yes, but I won't leave without my wife and my child.'

He called old Funga over. 'You explain it to him. He doesn't seem to understand.'

'Save your skin, Théoneste,' he implored. 'Don't be stubborn. You have the good luck of being Hutu, take advantage of it.'

'I'm willing to go home but with my wife and my child. That's what home is, right?'

'They're Tutsi, and Tutsis don't have any rights,' Nyumurowo dryly replied.

'Then I choose to stay here.'

He looked at my mother and me with sad eyes and turned toward the corporal. 'If I understand it correctly, you're going to kill us all?'

'You're not as stupid as they say,' sniggered the soldier.

'I thought you wanted to protect us. We've done nothing. We're going to defend ourselves.'

Nyumurowo hit him on the shoulder with his rifle butt. He swayed but didn't fall: there was no room to fall. People were packed in the halls, the offices, the storerooms, the kitchens, the bathrooms, crammed in the aisles, perched on the windowsills and above the confessional. We were so crowded that the sweat from on person's brow ran down another's nose. We were bumping into each other, we were suffocating, we were trampling each other. No one seemed to mind. The gestures were kind, the looks full of indulgence. And the silence was creating the same spell as a prayer of thanksgiving. The tear of a child tortured by the heat, the rattle of an old man asking for something to drink – knowing full well it was in vain – reminded me of the sudden interludes of the choir during the long Sunday Mass. My mother, her hands linked together above her head (that's how we mourn here), kept her eyes fixed on my father's jacket, now spotted with blood. I let out a few sobs then I began to holler.

'Shut up!' said Nyumurowo grabbing the kite from my hands. 'Look at this kid, he brought his kite! . . . You think we're here to play?'

A woman's voice could be heard from the other side of the altar.

'Chief, I have money and jewelry hidden in my mattress. I have a brick house and ten dairy cows. I'll let you have all that if you kill me right away. And with a rifle, please, not a machete!'

'As far as we're concerned, you're all Tutsis here. And we kill Tutsis the way we want!'

'It's obvious you don't understand the words of the ancients,' my father exclaimed with the same silly, happy grin as when he went to market or drank his palm wine. ''If you hate a man, let him live.' That's what the ancients said.'

Nyumurowo left without replying and, this time, he padlocked the door.

⋆ ⋆

We heard someone shout some orders. The stained-glass windows shattered, the icons crumbled to dust, dozens of mangled brains splashed against the ceiling and the walls. They were throwing grenades. My memory of the genocide stops here. The rest, I was told later, or it resurfaced on its own in my tattered memory, in spurts, like muddy water pouring out of a clogged pump. I don't know who died first, my father or my mother. Did they die from a grenade or finished off with machetes or hammers? When I regained consciousness, I noticed that their bodies were in pieces except my mother's chest whose breasts still in perfect condition were dripping with blood. An old woman was standing over me. She found the strength to smile at me amid the swarms of flies and the piles of decomposing corpses.

'I rescued one yesterday and one this morning,' she whispered. 'Both times, I thought I heard someone groaning but I wasn't sure. But once I was back home, I couldn't stop thinking about it, so I came back to make sure. I had to dig for a long time; I certainly didn't think it would be a child. You were gripping your mother like a newborn and you were nursing at her breasts. You're not a man like others. You were born twice in a way: the first time you were suckling her milk and the second time, her blood . . . Oh, God, three survivors, and seven days after the massacre! There's always some life left, even when the devil has passed through!'

96